THE WRITERS CIRCLE 2

Edited by

Nathan Primeau

&

Abigail Rabishaw

PRIME PRESS

Prime Press
contact@primepress.ca
www.primepress.ca

ISBN 978-0-99366-514-1 (perfect bound)

The Writers Circle Logo by Nathan Primeau
Prime Press Logo by Zak Hartong
Book Cover by Nathan Primeau
Book Design by Nathan Primeau
Map of Ybon by Logan Primeau
Printed in the United States of America

First Edition

14 13 12 11 10 / 10 9 8 7 6 5 4 3 2 1

COPYRIGHTS

All authors retain their individual copyrights for their entries,

and they are published here with their permission.

CONTENTS

NONFICTION

WHAT IS TWC?

The Writers Circle (TWC) is a community of writers who communicate with each other through social networks.

The Writers Circle 2 anthology has collected a series of stories and poems from The Writers Circle community and open submissions.

The selected entries exhibit various depictions of "ends". The freedom as to which sort of ends are presented within each contribution is at the discretion of the writers.

FICTION

IN THE END
MACKENZIE T. AGARD

Now in Death

He graces the market streets with his presence. Sauntering past a stubby, round merchant hollering about the superb sweetness of his cart's dates, he lifts an arm to adjust his nemes; the thin cloth of blue and gold absorbs the wig hugging his bald scalp. Continuing through town as dusk wraps the dusty earth in shadows, he finds his way to his resting chambers. Taking a moment to admire the painted figures occupying the walls and gold furnitures littered about the floor, he lies in his form-fitting sarcophagus and closes his eyes.

Then in Life

I slunk down the hallway, a mild breeze travelling a worn foot-path. My heart was in my ears, my pale, sienna skin peppered with sweat. My butter-yellow tunic hung in the crease of my elbow; I could feel his hands on my face, my thighs.

Now in Death

Gazing out into the tall, billowy grounds, he surveys their work. His body allows him to raise a hand over his eyes, promoting some reprieve from Ra's powerful, searing but fruitful rays. Thank goodness for his akh having once been acknowledged as the Great House; possessing an akh of royalty in the mortal world would now allow him to live the most prestigious afterlife. Proof of such was present in the flax fields before him; crouching, plucking, shuffling, groaning, sweating in Ra's hazy light, the roughly 120 field hands tended plot after plot of agriculture, working through the early morning and late afternoon.

Then in Life

My cot was a lumpy cage that night, too padded to be uncomfortable but too dark and lonely and barren to claim the opposite. Though plenty other brown-skinned, dark- haired girls lay peacefully in the cots around me, my mood in the harem felt full of aggravation and subdued dread. My role in the palace had recently shifted from rtpat to King's Wife; a transition from hereditary princess to a position marked with child-bearing responsibilities weighed on me, weighed on my

The Writers Circle 2

relationships. Once an open, thoughtful spirit, I lay in my bed with repressed confessions and deluded agendas fastened to my brain like the most brutal, constricting clamp. Curling my fingers into themselves I stared into the darkness, and when the kek overcame me, I fell asleep.

***

I eyed the large silver bowl of mixed lentils and cucumber. Breakfast with my family introduced the thick smell of stewed goat, the sweet smell of vegetables, and the warm scent of cooling bread, to the palace halls. As my favoured breakfast made its way around the table towards me, I passed a decorated water vase to my right. Mother, the Great Wife, Kekimhotep—only one of her many names described her accurately. As the primary wife to the Pharaoh, her ability to bear children was a basic, cardinal, and essential function; though her ability did not mean much if it produced no male heirs. *That's where I come in.*

***

I don't even know if she knows. The strain I had always felt as a child when I kept things from my mother was being released ten-fold on my psyche. The long, tan arms that used to embrace me each and every time I woke from a fitful sleep, the dark, low- hanging bangs I once wanted to emulate so badly I got one of my sisters, Lapis, to use the copper-bladed razor against my neat hairs—seemed so distant. Now, I felt so much worse in her presence, both too ashamed and scared to speak the truth with her.

But I can talk with Ebo. My beautiful, munefer, Ebo. He calms me, straightens me, grounds me. Telling him was hard too, of course. But we both knew when our fondness manifested seasons ago that ultimately, the options for my future were to bear children for a noble or marry foreign and make my place in another King's harem.

***

"Meryety Ebo, lovely Ebo, I'm here."

I paced the barley fields; after helping my sisters decide on the table arrangements and wall ornaments for the following day's banquet, I made my escape to the fields—neutral ground, for Ebo and I.

"I see you, love, your figure as enticing as ever."

Brushing away rough stalks as I went, I picked up my speed until I felt the nail of his largest toe beneath my bare feet, his chin against my forehead.

"Ah, it was hard as ever to sit with my mother upon Ra's rise today," I began. "I know it will do me some good to tell her, but is my good even worth her pain?"

"Well, not to play Apep's advocate, but your mother—knowing the responsibilities of Great Wife—is surely always aware that the Pharaoh may bear child with any woman from the harem. There is no—"

"That woman being her child, though, is..."

Confused thoughts left my mouth on a sudden, heavy wind passing through the fields.

"I realize it has shifted your relationship with her, but this deviation is not your fault. As always your beautiful intentions mimic Ra's—fair, thoughtful and influential. Nefermira, remember that your Ka is aptly named."

Now in Death

Before arriving in Duat he had been quite clear regarding his expectations of his afterlife, demanding that he be buried with at least 280 servants—perhaps more, but certainly no less. Only about two hundred had arrived in Aaru, the plot of Duat given to him by Ra. Though he griped constantly about the lack of help within his palace while he was alive, one must admit that sending 280 people to the Great God Anpu for the weighing of hearts against Ma'at's feather, undoubtably meant that it would take some time until all were processed.

Then in Life

"Finished."

"Your choices work well with what I knew of her, Nefermira. Simple, yet sharp and elegant, I'm sure the reunion of your aunt's Ba and Ka in the afterlife will be quite effortless; her akh will be proud."

I made my way back to the harem for a light, afternoon rest. Helping the servants and my family complete the finishing designs on my aunt's sarcophagus had been a tiresome affair. I was thankful for my sisters, who agreed to handle writing the list of servants expected to be sacrificed in order to aid my aunt in her afterlife. It would be sad to see Sabra go; she was the best seamstress in the palace and could fix a hem like no one else.

Now in Death

Finally, Ebo has arrived, his heart declared equal in weight to Ma'at's feather. In life he had been the Pharoah's right-hand man, bringing canteens of wine and platters of dates and figs whenever Khenemetkek called. He does not look forward to an eternity of servitude in Duat, in darkness and without Nefermira. Their separation had been imminent, but he feels as though no distance in his past life could ever mirror the misery feels in this death.

Then in Life

I was sitting against a pomegranate tree when

Kekimhotep came to see me, her pale-jade tunic wrapped around her body and the family's feline companion relaxed in her arms. Bending at the knees, then waist, she sat on a patch of thick grass to my left.

"I feel as though I've not seen you for days," she chuckled, a rough stone on a smooth blade. "Though I do suppose we have our morning meal together each day; we have not talked just the two of us in quite a while. I see my eldest daughter keeping the palace in order, her sisters in good health and her Pharaoh's spirits high; it is easy to be the Great Wife with the help you offer. Thank you, Nefermira."

Reaching over the cat, she touched my arm with cool fingertips. Keeping my father's spirits high, yes, that was why I'd often been too busy to see her. My mother's fingers wrapped gently around my forearm. Like mine, her palm was long, her wrist slender. Her hand was dry. It felt like his skin, dry beneath my hand that skimmed his abdomen. *His tongue touching my neck*— I gulped, determined to keep my face straight and my back against the tree's ragged bark.

"I heard that everything has been planned regarding your auntie's resting place. It really is a shame that she'll be taking Sabra with her. The magic that woman does on my hems..."

"She will be missed," I agreed, solemnly. "I am sorry Kekimhotep, but I feel quite drowsy and would like to rest before supper." I got to my feet and brushed dirt and grit from my tunic. She did the same, holding her arms around her torso. *His grip on my waist.* Looking down at the ground, I gave her a departing nod and scuttled back to the women's quarters.

***

I was woken from my first peaceful rest in days by one of my least favourite servants. Maleah was her name; too many times I'd caught her eyeing my amethyst hair pieces with the cunning expression of a devious opportunist. She did not have much to say, just that father requested me to his chambers again that night. It was the fifth time that week.

I was exhausted, irritated, confused, lonely, afraid, and sick of myself, but what the Great House demanded, the Great House received.

Now in Death

His favourite time of day is right after Ra retires for the evening. The darkness that evening brings signals the reunion of his Ba and Ka at his resting place. Though his Ba stays in Aaru during the long, hazy days of his life in death, his Ka visits his living family daily. This disconnect of soul—Ba and Ka—is still new to him; feeling uncomfortable about this dissonance, he starts to focus on the consciousness that his roaming Ka collects throughout the day. Falling asleep to visions of his family gives him a kind of peace he had not often experienced during his life. The memory of Kekimhotep's sleek, sleek hair and Nefermira's bright eyes, penetrate his relaxed imagination almost every night.

Then in Life

"Oh, dearest, there's one last thing."

Eight steps. Just eight more steps and I would have been through the door, far enough to pretend I did not hear when she called.

"Nefermira."

At the note of impatience in her voice I turned to face her. Her hair, straight and smooth as ever, fell over her right shoulder, swerved left into her cleavage, and hung over the front of her egg-white tunic, just above her belly button. I wondered if Ebo ever wished I had breasts like that, then took the thought back as quickly as it came about in the first place. A larger chest would only attract more attention from the Pharaoh; having a more ideal child-bearing body would not help my situation any.

"Nefermira, you better not be testing me."

I whipped my head up to meet my mother's eyes. She was clearly irritated, her lips teased away from her face.

"I apologize, Kekimhotep. My mind is foggy this morning."

"Well, I just wanted to make sure that you watch yourself around your father this morning; none of that 'mind fog'. Khenemetkek is in a horrible mood. Apparently, there was an incident last night in which Ebo dropped and broke your father's favourite wine vase and then just left it in pieces outside Khenemetkek's doorway. Coming out of his room this morning, your father cut his foot on a shard of it. When you help him plan his tour route for the Wag Festival, be quiet, patient and mindful of his aggravated state."

After the word 'dropped' passed her lips I heard nothing. I knew exactly what she was talking about; I had heard that crash with my own ears last night. I had been with Khenemetkek when he requested wine and dates be brought to his room and I asked to retire to the harem for the night. He denied my desire, annoyed at my rush to separate myself from him. *Ebo.*

"I think I've got to watch him more carefully," my mother's babbling forced its way to my consciousness. "He's been a little distant. He does not talk with me as much and has definitely been drinking and sleeping more than usual lately..."

"Mother, I will and I have to go." Ignoring her protest I ran to the servants' quarters, desperate to find out what he'd seen, how my new responsibility was bruising my relationship with

Ebo.

After requesting one of the male servants to bring Ebo from his cot only to learn that he was at the stables, I found him lying on a bail of grain, his strong chin turned to the sky.

"You were in Khenemetkek's chambers last night."

I did not flinch. I had been honest with him. There was nothing I could do to make it any better.

"I was."

"I know that I knew," his chin came down, but he still did not look at me. "I know that I knew," he repeated and opened his arms. *My Ebo, my lovely Ebo.*

***

And even after that critical moment with Ebo, the gods did not grant me even one moment of peace.

My mother found out that father was sleeping with other women from the harem with the intention of birthing a male heir.

She did not, however, realize that I was one of them.

In the afternoon, after she explained to me how she went into Khenemetkek's chambers to surprise him with some company in the late evening and found a noble's daughter with my father, I lay in the grass outside. I felt the most powerful god's heat crisp my skin and did not know whether to cry, die, or just keep lying there and wait for a miracle I knew would not come.

I was not sure how Ra could continue to nourish field upon field of grain, yet my happiness was decaying before my eyes.

***

Kekimhotep did not show any emotional reaction to the fact that though she stayed in the position of Great Wife, she was no longer in an exclusive relationship with my father. It is true that she was aware that this could be a possibility of her marriage from the beginning, but still, at the very least I expected her to show some anger; I knew that hidden behind the thick kohl streaks lining her eyes lay a fierce temper. I had seen it on numerous occasions and though I generally wished for no one to have to experience it, the fact that my father was the Pharaoh allowed him to be her one exception.

***

Several days later, after Ra had rose and sunk six times, the family was dining together and finalizing details for the Wag festival.

My mother and Khenemetkek were spending more time together again and my sisters and I were relieved. Not that their problems had much to do with us, but the less hostility there was between the two of them, the less there was to boil over at me and my siblings for absolutely no reason. Well, I suppose it would be justified in my case, but Kekimhotep did not know that.

The secret gripped me more than it had before, but there was no way I could confide in my mother after she made peace with the new responsibilities (or lack thereof) of her position in the palace. Besides, the strain of it all had torn my vocal cords from my throat; I barely spoke anymore, my thoughts locked away with unvoiced confessions.

Apparently the dates were also locked away with my confessions, none were presented with the wine and fruit at the end of our meal.

"Relax, dear," my mother rubbed my father's back. "I wanted to try a different spice on the dates as a special treat for the festival, so I made a platter with figs and such for you to taste later this evening."

How my gorgeous mother could still be—or even *pretend*, to be—kind to Khenemetkek, the Pharaoh, my father, was beyond me. But I gave her merit, the only other being I knew to be so nice, was Ebo.

Now in Death

He did not eat dates anymore. What was once his favourite flavour, his most prized kind of flesh, now reminded him of death and tasted like poison.

Then in Life

They found him amongst the vivid, lush fabrics of the pillows in his sleeping chambers. There was no indication of how exactly he had died. Some thought it was murder by suffocation with the hand-sewn head-cushions, others proposed that he accidentally choked on the pit of a fig.

I knew better, but I certainly was not going to say so. Add another confession to my locked-box.

Ebo and I spent the afternoon together, for once with no worries. My mother and the other nobles took care of the details for Khenemetkek's burial, and I got to find out how it felt to have *Ebo's* hands on my thighs, my fingers on his abdomen, his grip on my waist, *our* sighs echoing through my eardrums.

Now in Death

He watches his eldest daughter empty her breakfast into a worn wooden bucket for a week and a half before the palace physician announces that she is pregnant. Spending most of his days in Aaru drinking the most delicious grape-wine he has ever savoured, Khenemetkek demands the spirit of his right-hand servant, Ebo, to visit the palace and report the day's events to him when he is too tired to travel himself. He enjoys updates on the state of his kingdom and the growth of his son.

***

On days such as these, when Ebo is tasked with reporting the events of current life at the palace to his Pharaoh, he makes all of it up on his way back to the King's plot of Duat. Instead of doing as he is told, he stands in the barley fields—neutral ground for him and Nefermira—admiring the warmth of Ra's light and watching his son grow old.

REFERENCE GUIDE

TERM	MEANING (variable depending on period in Egyptian history)
Aaru	"Field of reeds"; an ideal paradise land within Duat
Akh	A complete person, whether living or dead. Composed of five elements: body, Ba, Ka, Name, and Shadow.
Anpu (Inpu)	God of embalming; God of death In Greek = Anubis
Apep	God embodying chaos; appears in art as a giant serpent
Ba	An individual's personality (prevails in death); second half of the soul
Duat	Underworld
Harem	Place where women sleep
Ka	An individual's unique life-force (prevails in death); one half of the soul
Kek/Kuk (Kkw)	Personification of (primordial) darkness; raising of night

Kekimhotep	Darkness with peace; darkness in peace
Khenemetkek	One who is joined with darkness
King's Great Wife	Pharaoh's primary wife
King's Wife	A wife in the Pharaoh's harem
Ma'at	Goddess representing truth, justice, balance and morality; decides if a person will successfully reach the afterlife.
Meryety	Lovely; charming
Munefer	Beautiful
Nefermira	Beauty like Ra (Re)
Nemes	A striped rectangular cloth of blue and gold worn by the pharaohs.
Pharaoh	The Great House; House of God
Ra (Re)	Sun god
Rtpat (f)	Hereditary princess
Sabra	Patient (modern translation)
Wag Festival	Celebrates the death and rebirth of Wesir (Osiris)

WARM BREAD
SARAH ASHTON

It was three in the morning when my phone started buzzing. There was only one person who would be calling me at this hour, so in a matter of seconds I had rolled over and answered the call.

"Is everything okay?" I asked.

"We broke up," he replied.

"How far away are you?"

"I'm in the lobby."

"Okay," I said as I sat up and rubbed the sleep out of my eyes. "I'll be there in a minute."

I hung up the phone and sighed. The apartment was quiet. Devon wasn't home that night and hadn't been home in a while, which I wasn't upset about; normally I'd have to listen to singing at all hours of the night. I quickly slipped out of bed and left my room. I grabbed a sweater off the couch before walking out into the just-as-quiet hallway. The only sound was the buzz of the fluorescent lights. I pushed the button for the elevator, and listened as it came to life, before creaking to a stop at my floor. The ride down was just as quiet as the wait. There wasn't much going on that early in the morning.

I saw him as soon as the elevator doors opened in the lobby. He was shivering and his face was red, I wasn't sure if that was from the cold or crying. He looked like an animal at the zoo, stuck behind the glass entrance, lonely and afraid, but he perked up when he saw me. I walked over and opened the door.

He collapsed onto me, and I held him as tight as I could. He was shaking.

"Do you want to talk about it?" I asked without letting go.

I felt him shake his head in response. I didn't push. Right now, he needed a distraction.

We walked over to the elevator and stepped in together. I pressed the button to the fourteenth floor, the very top, and we stood in comfortable silence as the elevator began to move.

"You're not wearing shoes," was the first thing he said to me.

I looked down. "I didn't have time to grab them."

"Well, then your feet are going to freeze on the roof."

"What? We're not going to the roof. Not in the middle of

December."

"But we always do," he whined.

"We did in the fall, but we have such different schedules now, so you haven't really been here since it was warm."

The elevator opened and we stepped out.

We walked back to my place and made ourselves comfortable in the living room, which was finally clean thanks to Devon being gone. He was sitting on the couch as I sat against the wall across from him, as far from him as I could possibly get. We talked about anything and everything. Movies we've seen, how we never see movies together anymore. The places we dream of going, and how many mountains there are in the world. He asked how my mom was, and I glared at him. We had been friends since the beginning of university, he should've known better than to ask about that.

"Do you have any food?" he asked after about an hour.

"Is that all I'm here for? Feeding you?" I asked smirking.

"That and getting to the roof, and you've already let me down with the latter."

I rolled my eyes. "I might have bread in the freezer, I can make you toast."

He nodded. "Please."

The freezer was mostly empty except for a bag of bread. It had two slices left and sat beside an empty ice cube tray. I

     The Writers Circle 2

didn't even have to look in the fridge. It was just as bare.

"I think all I have to put on it is butter," I say, closing the freezer with my shoulder.

"Does anyone even live here?" he asked, laughing.

I put the bread in the toaster, pushing down on the lever a bit too hard.

"Well, you know, I've been spending most of my time at Alex's place, so I didn't have to buy any food," I say hesitantly. "But, um, I won't be doing that anymore, so I guess I've got to get back to getting groceries for myself."

"What happened? When did this happen?" he asked.

"A bit over a week ago." I hesitate again. "I found out Alex had been cheating on me, so…"

"Why didn't you tell me?"

"You had your own relationship issues to deal with, you didn't need to deal with mine," I responded.

"Well –"

"And you're always so busy now, I didn't think you'd have time."

"But –"

"And what would you have done? Answer my call at three AM and invite me inside and make me toast?"

"That's not fair," he started, but then the toast popped. It was barely brown, so I flipped it over and pushed the lever back down.

"What's not fair?" I asked honestly. "I'm just telling the truth."

"I would –"

"No, you wouldn't," I cut him off. I tried to remain calm, but I couldn't stop myself from getting louder. "Because I tried. I did call you, not at three AM, but at a far more reasonable time of six PM and you said you couldn't talk because you were busy, and you said you'd call me later. So, I came home to an empty apartment, with very little food in it, and I made myself some toast and I worked it out myself, because you never did 'call me later.'"

The toast popped again.

There was an awkward pause.

"I'm sorry," he said without meeting my gaze. "You probably shouldn't be so loud; won't you wake up your roommate?"

"Devon?" I ask without looking at him. "No. Devon's at Alex's tonight."

We stood there together in silence. The toast remained untouched.

"I guess I should get going," he said, as he looked for his shoes.

"Aren't you going to eat your toast?"

"I can eat it on my way home."

"No," I say. "You can stay if you want to."

He paused. "Are you sure?"

"Yeah, you've had a long night. You can crash here."

He nodded and walked off to my room. I felt a pang of regret. I know he's using me, but I'm not sure if he realizes it. I give him way more than he gives me, and I always feel like I should let him go. But at this point, I'm too afraid of being alone. I can't lose him, not after Devon, not after Alex. So, I'll keep making him toast, and maybe one day he'll spare me cold bread.

SEA-SWALLOWED
CHRISTIE COCHRELL

"We all were sea-swallow'd"

(*The Tempest*)

Her father's caregivers called every day from Wiltshire that August, and there was a shipwreck.

Stella hadn't been ready for disaster—not so early, not yet. Unwelcome news usually came mid-morning. But when she bundled up to walk Bengal, despite feeling chilly and achy with a summer cold, she found not the usual quiet darkness but a disorienting tempest of helicopters, search and rescue vehicles, invasive lights.

Watching the commotion as she waited on the bluff for Bengal—Benjie—her Cardigan Welsh Corgi with his brindle (tiger-striped) coat, for once supremely indifferent to the human events, she heard the awful grating, grinding of the hull against the rock the fishing boat was hung up on, the pitiless waves, onslaught after onslaught, breaking it to pieces. The noise and morning cold and foretaste of fatality rasped on her tender skin, chafed even in her lambswool-hooded coat.

***

She tried to describe it to her father later, in their painfully unsatisfactory few minutes stretched out over an ocean.

"A *shipwreck*, Dad."

It would have interested him greatly even a few months ago. For years, after Stella's mother succumbed to the ovarian cancer, Paul had wanted to buy a boat. Cousins of his in Poole had a berth at the Quay, but the venture never got beyond a discussion or two.

Dorothy, Stella's older sister, took the phone from Paul, and said again "You've got to come," in her voice of unanswerable reproach.

"I *can't*, Dottie." She felt her heart grinding against the unforgiving rocks, like the fishing boat's hull. "You know that. It's a new semester." She was bound by her graduate studies in Ocean Sciences at UCSC, the two-year lease she'd signed to rent the room in Becca Ashley's nearly seafront house that looked out on the inner patio with long needles of pine and Teaching Buddha cast from grey volcanic ash.

***

Stella lay low most of the day, feeling awful. Bengal lay on the covers next to her. She'd put on comfy socks, and wrapped up in the homemade quilt Dorothy had made one almost-happy Christmas. Becca knocked on her door in early afternoon, offering honey custard with vanilla, lemon rind. Her news was all about the shipwreck, which—"having read too many Cornish mysteries"—she deemed terribly unromantic.

"No French brandy!" she exclaimed indignantly. "No Spanish gold doubloons, no ancient amphorae." The undistinguished fishing boat had run aground at 2 a.m. The pilot and his dog had walked to shore during low tide. There'd been no evidence of drug smuggling, like the numerous boats from Mexico the news mentioned, though rumor had it that a flotilla of empty beer cans floated off the wave-struck craft.

***

Paul used to tell his daughters stories about gin smugglers and Moonrakers in Wiltshire, thirsty wool merchants who hid pilfered barrels in church crypts, village ponds, and claimed to be gazing at the reflection of the moon therein.

He'd been a merchant seaman in his day, traveling to the West Indies, South America; had learned to conjure exotic spirits with spices, mangos, peppers, rum. With marriage he'd been beached, partially tamed. Combed and bustled off to church, even—where he honed his fine baritone and went on singing in the choir. He loved sea shanties too; in 2011 drove

to a shanty festival in Ellesmere Port with an old friend who'd

worked aboard ships with John Lennon's father.

For years Paul led ghost tours of Salisbury, Avebury. He

opened a Caribbean cafe and bar (offering "potions"), employ-

ing a feisty middle-aged Jamaican enchantress and her son

Marley, until the son started harassing Dorothy despite her

husband and baby. Paul went on to conduct general tours

around Wiltshire—Salisbury and Stonehenge most popular,

but also the Avebury Stone Circles, and the Palladian mansion

and Temple of Apollo at Stourbridge, the journey through the

gardens meant to recall Aeneas's descent into the underworld.

Paul liked to compare himself with Tennyson's Ulysses,

always roaming with a hungry heart. But these past weeks

he'd learned "How dull it is to pause, to make an end," and had

followed the sinking star home to his arid bed—tended by

women émigrés far removed from their shores; and by

Dorothy, when three rambunctious children allowed.

***

That evening, walking Benjie, Stella saw the boat wreckage

further reduced. She listened on headphones to Strauss's Four

Last Songs, which she had heard in May in San Francisco with

her friend and lover Clay, before he'd left to take the job in San

Diego. She looked out at the fog shrouding the coast of Monterey across the bay, and thought of the Flying Dutchman, the man doomed never to make land.

Paul's doom was just the opposite. He'd left his seafaring for good, only reliving it through his collection of Patrick O'Brian books, *100 Years Before the Mast*, and a new translation of *Argonautika*. His confined flat was without sails, had had no rudder since their mother died. Nothing had come of his unrealistic dream of living on the historic lightship, which had caught his eye three or four years ago.

Even the flat was going, now. Dorothy had cleared out books and spices ruthlessly, had settled him in the back bedroom of their semidetached house in the Swindon suburbs.

***

Stella couldn't bear to think of him failing daily.

All week along the oceanfront she watched ongoing salvage operations—helicopters, divers, a crane to lift the wrack washed up into the tide pools and against the sandy bluffs. The boat's diesel fuel had seeped out; experts feared contamination in the bay; danger to seals, sea otters, pelicans, the two delightful oystercatchers with their bright orange beaks.

She confided everything to the dispassionate Buddha in his evergreen shrine, who she considered sage, mentor. Since Clay had gone, she'd felt cut off, alone. Dorothy relentlessly nagged at her to come home. Her father said nothing, but his confusion, the unbridgeable distance between them, was re-proof enough. She hummed the Scottish folk song he had liked, had sung quietly in his kitchen, seasoning Jamaican rice and peas, the night before she left for California—brave new world.

The water is wide, I cannot get o'er
Neither have I wings to fly

Her humming lament broke up, choked by salt tears.

***

Oceans were in both of them, she told the listening Buddha. She'd liked to think she was Stella, star of the sea. She'd liked to think she was Miranda, Prospero's daughter, sea wrought. After a traveling troupe of players visited Winchester and they all fell in love with the magic of Shakespeare's island play, Paul told ten-year-old Stella that Shakespeare's tale was likely inspired by a real catastrophe. The year before he wrote it English ships supplying the Bermudas, a new colony, ran into "a cruel tempest," probably a hurricane.

***

All week she waited for the phone call ending it. Tides played indifferently with vestiges of wreckage still below the bluff. Benjie followed phantom whiffs and whispers through the coastal prairie grass. Across the wide water, the fast approaching dark, Stella caught a glimmer of transient lights. The Flying Dutchman finally making land, she thought. Helping an indistinct figure on board.

CODA
MICHAEL HARRIS COHEN

Left Ventricle

Only Borges has seen the structure from the outside so they rely on his descriptions, strange as they are. He roams where he pleases, except for the head. He wanders, returns and depicts. Still, the system brought him back blind and they wonder: can his reports be trusted?

"My fellow writers," Borges says. "We dwell in the ideal man—Adam Kadmon. People reside in the limbs and torso. The fingers and toes. We live in the heart of this celestial construction."

"Live?" Faulkner says. "This ain't much like life."

Borges turns to the voice. He smiles at Faulkner. He palms back his own silvery hair. "William, it is exactly like life."

The writers adapt to the heart theory. It makes sense as much as anything makes sense here. Walls and ceilings curve, hallways twist like mole tunnels. No corners exist.

Entombed within a Heart—could be, Emily supposes. She'd imagined death differently, but is flexible.

But if death is a heart it is massive. No one has counted all the writers in their rooms but there are hundreds. Possibly thousands. If this is a heart, how big is the man?

Left Atrium

Borges' stories of the feet and hands convince some. In these parts, according to him, the occupants work all the time. Not like the writers. The writers do as they please. They can stare at the blank-white walls, ceilings, and floors all day. Most do.

"The feet and hands are restless," Borges says. "Filled with doers. Napoleon charges. Magellan explores. Alexander conquers. There is no peace. One might call the feet hell and the head heaven. Our home, the heart, is purgatory."

"Aphoristic," Faulkner says.

"Exactly. He's writing out loud," murmurs Baldwin. "You know his work?"

Faulkner pats his mustache. "Not my cup of tea."

"Well I know it. Motherfucker is writing a story. Don't trust it."

As for the head, where Borges cannot travel, he calls it

Keter. "Nothing there," Borges says. "Nothing that one can understand."

Septum

But rumors persist. The longer dead veer religious. Donne says the head is crowded with angels. Alighieri pronounces the opposite. Verne pontificates a dirigible with human features. Burroughs suggests a machine run amok, an aimless thing that views writers as insects.

Austen has another theory. "I know many of you, but the one I know best is absent," she says.

The writers look around. Who is missing?

"Melville?" Faulkner shouts.

"In his room," says Beckett. "Writing. Failing, better and better."

"Maybe we should all be writing?" Tolstoy says. "The act of creation brought us in. Perhaps it is the means out."

Joyce looks around. "Fuck me with a tree rat," he says.

"Tree rat?" Nin says.

"Squirrel," says Steinbeck.

"Not here," says Joyce.

"Who?" they shout in unison.

"Him," Joyce whispers as Austen nods and smirks.

Right Ventricle

Faulkner rolls his eyes and yanks the sheet from his typewriter. He wads it and tosses it over his shoulder. The ball lands at Emily's feet. She unfolds the paper, smoothens it, and tucks it in her dress.

"If that's true," Faulkner says, "If that fella's back at work upstairs, ain't no use for the rest of us."

Dostoyevsky wrings his hands and nods. Celine scowls. Rimbaud spits in the corner, though no spit comes. The system stopped the necessity to excrete. "That's why we can't write," Poe has said before and will say again. "Words are excretory functions for the head."

"Nothing left to do but drink," Hemingway says. He fills Faulkner's glass, then his own. Whiskey, or it's supposed to be. It looks and tastes right but never gets one drunk. Capote calls it "Fool's Gold," though he slurps martinis day or night—or whenever it is—even if the gin tastes, in his words, "Contrived."

The rumor grows: He'd brought them back. He runs the head, the show, using all of them. The Bard is the system.

Right Atrium

Borges smiles noncommittally. He changes the subject, sketches the science: "An infinitesimal piece. That's all they

needed. From grains of sand they recreate the universes of us."
He taps his cane three times on the floor. "Science. Magic.
Alchemy."

Poets stir in their corner, recalling bridge leaps and ovens
without flame. Hemingway contemplates what he left behind
on a shotgun-spattered wall. He touches the back of his head,
a new tic; it's whole skulled and fully haired. Joyce reminisces
seed spent on Italian hotel sheets.

"To what end?" Goethe asks. "Why continue to live when
we have died? What is life without end?"

"The point of life is that it ends," chirps a voice from the
back. "And this is not life." Kafka. Snuck in like a rodent. He
blushes when they turn his way.

Borges clasps his hands together and smiles—always smiling that Borges. "Yes, here the end has no end."

Borges tries to raise morale with stories of the philoso-
phers. "Broken epistemologies suffocate them. It's panicked
and contentious in the belly. Escape tactics war with screeds.
Plato and Popper endlessly argue. Kierkegaard sobs. Heideg-
ger Daseins."

He tells them again of the painters and musicians. "We're
neighbors. Brothers closest to the heart. Picasso knows infi-
nite stories. Mozart fashioned a lute from wig hair and a bit of
pipe. Even Goya dances. Music is their clock."

     The Writers Circle 2

"¿Pero realmente pintan?" Marques asks.

Borges smiles. "They paint, of course. They paint the room with laughter."

None of the writers are laughing.

"We must write," Woolf says again. "There is nothing else."

Aorta

And so they do. They return to their rooms or gather at the long tables. They fling words down, waiting for shape to emerge.

Only Emily stands to the side. She smiles inscrutably. The word on her lips is the same word in all their mouths, though none dare write it. Eternity.

POLK THE PILOT
NICHOLAS FORSTER

Defenders streaked across the heavens, burning bright lines in his retina. Polk's replacement eye followed its partner, the vision less powerful than before, straggling in focus and image capture.

"Did you see that?" Polk asked his companion. Fleet yawned and rubbed his forehead, brushing back the black, greasy hair. "Yes, Polk, I saw them."

Fleet's voice betrayed his enthusiasm, not sharing the zeal Polk had for the plentiful spacecraft. The streets of Lack with its rows of dingy habitation pods spread before them, covered by the dome in front of the mountains of the moon.

Polk followed their path with his gaze. Beyond the fading chem-streaks, the blue, white globe poked over the peaks, in another stunning Earthrise. Polk and Fleet were up this early most days, as the shift at the plant ended at 5:55 Lunar

Standard Daytime.

"Don't sweat it, pal, flying is probably not as great as it looks."

Fleet's astute observation took Polk back in time. Dad knew how to state the obvious, too. After Mom died in San Fran, he managed Polk's dreaming ways. Now his friend took up the reins. "It's not that you couldn't fly those things with one eye, it's that they won't let you. Don't beat yourself up."

Polk lowered his head and kicked the dusty road. With fingers rubbed raw from the scrubbing, he scratched the scarred socket above the mechanical replacement. "It works sometimes," he said, tapping the orb thrice above the iris. "There!"

A crackled, black-and-white image appeared of Fleet's six-foot-two gangly form, and depth perception returned. "See, it's not that bad."

Fleet frowned and patted Polk's back. "Ya, I know it ain't terrible, Polky. Let's get something to eat." The two followed the row of pods out toward the fringe of Lack, where the nourishment centers and the supply depots ringed the junction of the domes.

A disheveled creature scurried out before them. Polk reached down to intercept, and its eyes reflected the dim earthlight. "Go home now, Fleabag, we'll bring you some scraps when we come back."

The resourceful feline sat on the path behind them, one torn ear perked up, the other flopped. Polk had found him after the accident, and the two looked after each other ever since. Besides Fleabag, only Fleet and Homar seemed to take any notice of Polk. The former in a similar situation, orphaned and alone on the base. The latter, though in it for himself, extended tidbits and morsels to Fleet and Polk in times of need. They passed his pod now, the glow from within denoting his presence, but they wouldn't dream of disturbing him unannounced.

The two walked in silence through the dusty streets of Lack, following the concentric lines between the pods. More defenders shot overhead, darts across the ink black of space. Littered moon cards dotted the ground and the hive-openings of the parts district. Robot stores loomed before them, and Fleet stopped and nudged Polk.

"Check it out, buddy." A big grin on his face and his blue eyes sparkling. "With that you could see alright."

Polk looked to the window in the structure Fleet motioned toward. Inside, on a red ruby pillow sat a marvelous eyeball, smooth, perfect, white with brown iris and black pupil. The eye did not look misshapen or greyed, like the malfunctioning Lack-town replacement Polk wore. This was the

The Writers Circle 2

real deal.

"There'd be nothing stopping you from attending Defender academy with that in, Polky-boy."

Polk stepped to the door of the storefront and peeked in. The place was empty. The magnificent orb just sat there, an arm length away. All he had to do was reach out and take it, and they could run. His heart beat in his chest. With nerves tighter than the tension wires at the scrub house, he waited and looked around at the racks and shelves. No cameras. No attending robots. No attendant.

"I can't do it."

"Excuse me?"

"One thing I promised Dad before he died… I wouldn't steal."

Fleet laughed and pulled on Polk's silversuit. "Come on man, I wasn't asking you to steal it! You think you'd escape the notice of the sensors? Let's get out of here."

Polk scrunched his face and looked around the shop, shamed by his uncontrolled outburst. Though just a poor parts scrubber in the slums of Lack, he was no thief. "Hold up, I want to find out about this thing," Polk said. He went in and called out in a clear loud voice, "Hello, is anybody here?"

A portly, bald man stepped out beyond a curtain in the back. He wore a golden tinfoil garment, and his tapered lengthy eyebrows curled upward. He cocked one eye and cast a dubious look. Polk noticed his reflection in the metallic walls and remembered his scruff.

"Are you looking for something in particular?" A shrewd glance at the orb on the pillow made Polk think he knew damn well what they were looking at. His vision crackled in the right, causing a static snowstorm of grey, then returned.

"The eye," Polk said, somewhat embarrassed. "How much?"

Fleet tugged at Polk's suit and under his breath muttered, "Forget it buddy. Come on, let's go."

The shopkeeper's demeanor changed; a gleam replaced the doubt. The dealer's face transformed with a wide smile and the curved eyebrows curled. "Why didn't you say so! I see you need an eye, don't you?"

"Well, you are looking at the finest sphere in the field of vision repair in all the solar system. The android dealers and the prosthetics deployers keep these rolling off my shelves. This is one of the last ones I have left."

Polk frowned. He didn't like where this was headed and thrust his hands deep in the silversuit pockets. "How much does it cost?"

"For you, my good man, 1000 moondogs."

Deflated, Polk's breath left him and his shoulders drooped.

What were you thinking? You're a scrubber. You can't buy scat. He turned and followed Fleet out the doorway. "Thanks, I'll have to see," he said, meek and quiet as a pauper in a playhouse.

Conversation was subdued as they munched on the replication burgers. Polk felt stupid for entertaining such lofty aspirations. But even so, hope lurked in the background of his mind. He'd been saving credits ever since he started earning and had a stash at the pod. He grabbed a sack of the food scraps to bring back for his little friend and they left.

They walked home and Polk said goodbye.

"Don't worry about the eye, Polky-boy, Fleet said, winking. "You'll get your chance one day. Catch you before the shift."

Polk smiled in response and shuffled behind his pod where the entrance disc whisked open. Fleabag usually waited for him there, but not tonight. With the eyeball still on his mind, Polk raced for his storage locker. Deep inside lay his portfolio of credit, which he kept nestled beneath the small portion of memory stickles from his parents. He ripped the cover to the skein to reveal the credits and counted them. Nowhere even close to what he needed.

He shrank down to the seat and unzipped the front of the silversuit, throwing the moondogs on the bed. What was I thinking! He thought again and opened the door.

"Fleabag!" he yelled into the night, then muttered to himself. "Where is that damn cat?"

***

Polk barely slept, his fake eye buzzing every few minutes, and rather than endure the mechanical buzz, he turned it off. The weight of the useless metal in his face caused an irritation not only to his skin, but to his soul.

With weary legs, he trudged off behind Fleet toward the docks for work and pondered the futility of it all. Scrubbing Petrick cores barely kept him alive, and regardless, it would end soon. The Asteroid Defender 211s were coming, rendering the I-otta 500s obsolete. The improved spacecraft ran on a completely new technology and the parts he knew would be gone.

Polk saw no way out of poverty and would never get to be a pilot. He had to try something better, quicker. He needed to go find Homar.

"Tell them I'm sick today, Fleet," he called out after his friend. "Say I have the stomach squirts. The controllers never question that."

Fleet turned and held his head to the side. "It's your life, man, but don't be surprised if they won't take you back. There's plenty of greasers in Lack looking for your job."

Polk didn't care. The futility of scrubbing for the measly moondogs he'd earn was sucking the last bit of life left in him. He couldn't face one more day, and if they didn't let a guy with stomach squirts stay home, they weren't worth working for.

Homar's turnoff was a few rows behind, and Polk turned and ran back the other way. He slid past the other workertons and bound down the alley towards his pod. As if sensing his arrival, the door opened, revealing the lanky frame of Lack's finest Go24 men, perhaps the most renown in all of Moon Base One.

"Well, if it isn't Zitar's boy," he said with his Southy drawl. "Shouldn't you be down at the docks? Wouldn't want anyone to get the finger on you."

Polk bit his lower lip and ramped up the courage. Homar helped his dad and he when they first got to Lack. Pops never said what he did, but the boost earned him the pod and a job at the scrubber docks. Without him, they'd have been shipped back down to the planet, to endure the dry lands or worse. He lowered his gaze and said quiet-like, "Homar, I need some help. I have to get enough credits to buy a new eye."

Homar grinned and hiked up his suit. "Well then, Polk-er-oo. Have I got a job for you!"

Polk smiled, the enthusiasm catching, and he started to believe he'd made the right choice. He forgot about the brass down at the scrubbers. They'd understand, and probably wouldn't even notice he was gone. Homar ushered him inside and with a glance left and right, shut the front door.

"There is a task I have for you today. It pays five times as much as scrubbing, and we'll have that eyeball in place in no time." Homar paced the room and began to explain. "You see, the moon cards that store the moondog credits over in Regard are thrown away after use. Robot rent and operation is based on it, and they literally pave the ground."

Polk recalled the discarded plastic cards that littered the streets of the upper-class zone. There were so many of them, they blended into the grey dust of the packed moon surface.

"Recon and regroup division are paying me big-time for the cards, but I can't get them fast enough for anyone. This is where you come in."

Homar sat down and steepled his fingers. "Collect them before the cleaners do and bring them back here. There is a way to reload the moondogs, rendering the discards at seventy-seven percent. I know a guy."

Polk listened with intent. This had to be legit, and he was seeing credits dance before his eye. He'd trudged through hundreds the other night in Regard. "Ok, I'm in. Tell me what I need to do."

"Well, little friend," Homar said with a smile, "all you have to do is get them for me."

***

Polk should have known nothing was as easy as it seems and retrieving the moon cards was anything but. It had only been an hour, and moondust coated him head to foot. The thin plastic chips stuck to the dirt, and getting them up required digging his nails in under the flattened pieces. He had no tools and no gloves, and the dry dust built up under his fingernails.

He shoved them in his pocket, making a notable bulge in his silversuit. His back hurt from stooping over, throat raw, and his fingers became dry and cracked.

"Out of the way, dust mite," a Regard citizen croaked as he hurried past Polk. "Shouldn't you be at the docks or at the plant, anyway?"

The scrubber docks were bad, but the plant was worse, and Polk looked up with scorn at the rear of the Regardian, as he loped off into the distance.

"Shouldn't you be at the plant?" Polk muttered under his breath after the well-to-do man.

As he watched him disappear up ahead, he caught his reflection in the shiny wall of the mineral expansion housing. The tin of a hanger door displayed his disheveled self. Dust mite was an appropriate moniker. His silversuit was grey with moon dust, his hair caked, and his glass eye was on the fritz, googling left and right, up and down.

"Hup now, hup," the words preceded the marching beat of the squad. Twenty Defender pilot trainees in formation streamed past him. Polk turned aside, hiding himself and his shame at having stooped so low. These would be his future contemporaries if he were to get the eye. He couldn't let them see him like this, so he shielded his face into his dirty suit and coughed, averting his eye and covering his glare. "Hup now, harry!" the lead defender called.

Polk had had it. He wouldn't shlep plasti-cards from the ground anymore, especially since they'd ultimately be used for nefarious purposes. The withered reflection spoke back to him. "Go back to work, dumbass. Leave those friggin things in the dust!"

With sudden realization, he regretted talking to Homar and taking on this ridiculous task. Picking up the discards of the citizenry felt on a lower level than begging. And he was no beggar. He'd worked hard all his life, and despite his messed-up, fake eye, he wouldn't stoop to being a scavenger.

Polk strode back the way he had come and passed the hive shop, the one with the eye, and there it was again. He stopped and looked at the store, his reflection ghost in front of the shining orb. His grimy disheveled suit, bulging at the pocket with moon chips, his mechanical eye on the fritz, going back and forth, up and down, not picking up any images except crackling static.

Again, he considered taking it. One quick grab and run. That's all.

He thought of Fleet at the Scrubber dock. He should be there, too, not picking plasti-moon cards out of the dust, not contemplating thievery at the robot parts store. He took one more wistful glance at the gleaming eye, and turned towards home, just as three defender ships shot overhead.

***

Homar didn't mind that he quit. He let out a little chuckle when Polk showed up only an hour after he'd left. The heap of chips from his pocket fetched 35 moondogs, which was a little more than he'd have made at the scrubber docks, but not worth the anguish it caused.

"Come back tomorrow, kid, just gotta bring me back those chips."

Polk pretended to smile, waved, and walked on by on his way home. He had to write this one off as experience. He would not sacrifice everything, his dignity or his pride, rolling around in the dirt trying to be someone he's not. There had to be another way.

Fleet wouldn't be back for hours and he reached his pod ready for a cleanup. Polk had moondust everywhere. He washed down in the water globule and dried off in the blower vent. He came out and put on a fresh silversuit. Hope they understand down at the docks, he thought, realizing his job wasn't the worst thing in the world. He'd survive despite not being a pilot and he would live, with his friend Fleet next door, and his cat, Fleabag, at his side.

The telltale sound of something rolling along the floor woke him from his thoughts. AD 201s roared across the sky. Fleabag pounced, then swatted the sphere again, where it skittered across the floor and under the furniture.

MINE ALONE
NATASHA KIRMSE

You were mine.

Mine and mine alone.

Those cold nights, I would sit awake, wide-eyed, struggling to feel something. I would fight off those tears, those pangs in my heart. I'd take in the frozen air, feeling it charge my lungs with a numbness I prayed I'd retain forever. I would hug myself tightly and envision it was you in my arms. I would hear your laugh, picture your smile, your brilliant brown eyes, the same shade as your father's, and his before him. I would talk to you. I felt as though you would understand. You would know the struggle I was going through, the attempt to get through every day, every moment, every breath…

It was suffocating.

I'd had attacks before. All my life. But you made them better. You gave me a purpose to stay grounded. To live.

I'd hear your voice, how it changed each day. It deepened when concerned, or grew lighter with laughter.

I was ready for a life with you. I was ready to have you by my side as we grew together, one of us aging faster than the other. I was ready to see steps, hear bells, feel your hand in mine through it all. I was ready to hold you in my arms, have our eyes meet, and know that I'd found the love of my life...

But it didn't work out that way.

Because with that sudden pain, that ache in my body, came the knowledge that something was wrong. With the pain came fear of the loss of the future I had planned. The future with you. With the pain came blood, nurses, doctors. With the pain came the expression we pray we'll never hear ---

I'm sorry for your loss.

Repeated, over and over. Sorry, so sorry for my loss. For my pain. Sorry I had to lose you before I could even truly have you, before I could meet you.

But they were wrong.

I did meet you.

I met you with every kick, every flutter. You moved in me, grew in me, and as such, I knew you more than any soul could ever know another. You supported me through my pain, through my sorrows. You kept me fighting as I pushed through the loneliness and the sickness. You made me care for myself as I never had before. Because it was no longer about me. It was about us. The moment I learned of you my life changed in a way I prayed would never stop. I felt light. I felt hope. I felt love. You were my answer.

You were mine.

And now you're hers. Your ashes spread over her, becoming one with her as spring continues to grow. You'll lie amongst flowers, trees, the life that connects us throughout the world. You'll be seen in every blossom, and as the winter slowly covers us, she'll hold you close and keep you safe until the warmer months beg for you to grow once again. Your life will no longer be limited by years, with danger always lurking. Not caught up in the fear and concern we humans always create. Instead, you'll grow with peace. You'll bloom as you never would have before. She knows you as you grow.

But I knew you as you formed. I knew the feeling of completion, of finally being whole. I knew the unconditional love I held for you and the love I was sure you returned despite you not knowing what love was. You loved me. And I loved you. And long as I live, I will feel those bubbles, that flutter, those kicks. I will picture the eyes I know you possessed. I will imagine your grips, your voice, your smile, your laugh... and I will ache for a life that once was - that could've been. But I will know that you are cared for. You are loved. And although I may not have you by my side

You are mine.

THE RAIN BEFORE THE STORM
BRICE PETERS

We're all such fucking parasites. Always living for the next experience, the next big thrill, the next high, riding on the coattails of someone else's adventures. We get to be the authors of our own destinies, but that doesn't mean we get to be our own heroes. Sometimes we're the background character in someone else's story. Sometimes, we're the villain. We write our own stories, make our own choices, but we don't always get to pick the genre. Sometimes you luck out and get a happy ending. Or, you'll end up like me. Stuck in a spiralling tragedy, without knowing or controlling how it ends.

***

The alarm shrieked into the darkness of my apartment. Instinctually, still half asleep, my arm reached out, slamming the alarm into silence. I opened my eyes. A quick glance showed the time, three-thirty in the goddamn morning. With a deep breath, I reluctantly sat up and prayed to the unknown that I'd somehow be overcome with illness, so I could call in sick.

With no miracle illness in sight, I got up. My feet dragged across the floor, shuffling about as effectively as the dead. I felt along the bathroom wall for the light switch. The snap of it being flicked on brought with it a searing pain to my retinas, as the peaceful darkness was washed away by the blinding light.

After a few seconds of blinking away tears and adjusting to the sudden brightness, I caught a glimpse of myself in the mirror. Disgusting. Total disaster. Unkempt, mousy hair in every direction, green eyes sunken deep into pale flesh, highlighted by the bruise-like bags under each socket. For 27, I looked like shit. A decade older at best, a ghost of myself at worst.

As I started the shower and let the scorching water pour over me, I obsessed over the mirror. The mirror always did a great job of stripping down any façade I had of myself. I was no hero, no handsome protagonist I tried to see myself as. When it came down to it, the mirror never lied. And I hated what it showed me.

The harsh shriek of the alarm echoed through my apartment again.

"Fuck," I muttered. "Must've hit snooze again."

I shut off the shower with anger, storming out to the crisp

air of my apartment. as I had to leave the comfort of the hot water and step out into the cool crisp air that filled the apartment.

I left the bathroom, and entered the living room in this miserable apartment. It was lit only by the light from the bathroom. I walked through the poorly lit room and turned on the light for the living room, that's when I saw Jenna stand in the doorway of the bedroom, saying nothing just staring at me. Her long black hair blended in with the darkness, her green eyes seemed to glow like two fireflies in the night, illuminating her smooth beautiful skin. I returned the gesture by saying nothing in return, moving across the living room and past her into the bedroom and silencing the alarm. I doubted that the alarm didn't wake her, because I swear she never slept.

Mine and Jenna's relationship was toxic. It started out alright, maybe a little quick, but, like gas to a bonfire, our love was intense. Destructive. I was obsessed. I wanted to be with her all the time. This was a different kind of want, possessive, and overwhelming. I still don't know how best to describe it. I was on fire, engulfed in the flames of misery, and she was the water, there to save me. But, as time went on, my obsession with Jenna became all-consuming. Time without her became my biggest fear. I could barely function without her by my side. When she entered a room, it was like I knew everything would be okay, and nothing else mattered. Whenever I heard her say my name, asking me to come to her, that she needed me, my heart would skip a beat like a rock skipping on water, and inevitably I heeded the call no matter the circumstance. Whether I was at work, with friends, at a family dinner, I would leave to be with her.

At some point, I realized I had lost control. I wasn't even living for myself, I was living to be with her. I knew I had to end it. My family missed me. I hadn't seen them in months. When I called my mom to tell her I was ending things with Jenna, she cried out of happiness. She said she felt like she was getting her son back.

However, it wasn't quite that easy. Even though it had been months since I broke up with Jenna, she was still living in my apartment. And it wasn't for lack of trying. God, I had tried. I had begged and pleaded and screamed at her to just fucking leave already. But, she wouldn't. So, until I moved away, left the city, found a new place as far from her as physically possible, I was stuck.

She loved living with me still. It was like a constant temptation. Every time I saw her it was like she was telling me how easy it would be to just go back to her.

I glanced quickly at the clock, four-thirty, it was time to leave. I threw on my uniform and steel toes, and left.

I walked to work every morning, as I had for the past year. Rain or shine, I would walk from my apartment, through the forest, and arrive at work. Today was no different; I began my walk to work.

I enjoyed this morning ritual. It was peaceful, almost. I always cut through the nature sanctuary a few streets over, and it was like entering a different world.

The entrance of the forest itself looked like an arched doorframe, made from leaves of overlapping trees, with only darkness as a door. The beginning of the gravel path I took was barely visible. I took a deep breath of fresh air and ventured into the woods, finally feeling fully awake.

While the sanctuary was beautiful during the day, it was eerie in the early morning darkness. In the dark, the beauty of the plants and trees were lost, all the blooming, thriving life, clouded in shadows. I was sure other, more sinister things dwelled in the forest behind the flowers, but it was impossible to know in the dark. The very winds that rushed through the leaves at night sounded like whispers of lost souls who wandered in the woods and never found a way out. The forest always made me recall memories of reading horror stories about a monster in the woods. There was always that idiot who ventured into the dark for some reason, of course, they would have no cell phone signal or way to call for help. Any time I was alone in these dark woods, I felt like I was that same idiot.

That hour-long walk to work every morning inevitably filled my head with daydreams and a constant stream of thoughts.

Today's were all about Jill. Normal enough, given my situation, but it was like she possessed me every time she entered my head. I swear I would hear footsteps behind me whenever thoughts of her came up. This would be having me thinking she was walking behind me, lurking like a predator in the night, stalking its prey.

I would daydream about how my life was going to change, how it would be so much better when I escaped it all. How I would take control of my destiny and become the man I chose to be. Often times when my daydream ended, I would look around and just lose the will to try and control any part of my destiny. It felt hopeless.

As I emerged from the woods, I could see the warehouse I worked in at the end of a string of box stores.

I checked my phone. Five thirty. I had fifteen minutes to get to work. I quickened my walk, passing by each store, each ally, focused on getting to work on time, until-

"Hank."

I stopped and turned my head, searching for the source of the voice.

I hated this place and its shadowy alleys. Nothing good ever happened in a dark alleyway.

My phone began buzzing, breaking me out of my trance. It was my last alarm, telling me I should be at work by now.

I ran away from the alley to the warehouse, temporarily forgetting the voice. Made it just in time.

I clocked in and began my shift. My day was filled with menial tasks, essentially moving boxes around.

"Absolutely riveting" I muttered, shoving a box from one shelf to another. "What a good use of that biology degree."

The thought of my wasted time in university plagued me this morning. So many hours at the library, studying for the next exam, the endless working on laboratory reports for classes, and the death of my athleticism, all for nothing. I felt the empty void in me begin to consume all feelings of happiness I could or would feel. I began to slow down my work, the void consumed every bit of motivation to work or even be here.

"Hank!" My pity party was interrupted by my manager, Jackson. "Go help Stevens in the back, he needs a forklift spotter."

I nodded in response, then headed back.

"Stevens!" I shouted, my mood lifting already. I was so happy to have a friend like him at work. I had known him since kindergarten, and our morning chats were the highlight of my days.

"Hey there Hank!" Stevens called out in response.

"How goes it, amigo?" I shouted back.

Stevens just smirked and shrugged his shoulders. "You here to help out an old man?"

We were nearly thirty, but Stevens still acted like a teenager.

Stevens was standing beside the forklift, with two portable sheds hoisted above the ground on the forks of the lift, strapped to a large wooden pallet. Each box had to weigh at least a hundred and fifty pounds.

I headed down the aisle to where the sheds had to be placed, maybe 12 feet above our heads.

Stevens walked toward me, with a look on his face that told me he wasn't ready to actually work yet. We did that often, take these little unofficial breaks to make our shifts more bearable. We would talk anything, from what kind of kingdom we would run if we were kings in medieval times, to current political issues. Today it looked like Steve wanted to be serious.

He looked at me and sighed, "They threw a rock through my apartment window last night."

I sighed and squeezed my eyes shut while lowering my head. I knew that Stevens had trouble, Particularly with money. He liked to gamble, nothing to him matched the thrill of the cards. He was good at it too. I went to the Casino with him from time to time, and I had seen him sit at the Black Jack table for only an hour, and make a thousand dollars. It wasn't luck, he strategized and thought over every possible outcome and then he went in for the kill, betting big.

I didn't know where the hell he got his money to bet. I barely made enough for rent and groceries at this place working full time. Unfortunately for Stevens, he had a pretty critical weakness when it came to gambling, he was greedy. His eyes would widen when he sat at the tables, and the normal cheerful aura that he projected would darken and his eyes changed. They became cold; you could even describe them as cruel. Like a man who would do anything to satisfy his own yearning of owning whatever was worth anything. If he smelled the money, then he would place his bet and wait like a mad dog salivating at the scent of meat until the money was presented to him. When he lost he changed again. He got hungrier to win that next hand, he would get angry, I swear his eyes would turn red. I once saw him lunge at the dealer, it looked like he was gonna strangle him. It took every bit of strength I had to haul out Stevens while he cursed and screamed at everyone who would stop and listen. Needless to say, we were banned from the Casino in town for life. That led Stevens to try to find a new place to gamble.

From what he told me, he went out to a bar a week ago where there was a poker game. Stevens inevitably wanted in the game. The idiot didn't think twice since cards and money were involved. He didn't look past the table or the cards. He didn't think about going to a private room in the back of a bar, he didn't think when any of them asked if he was a cop, he just didn't think. The guys that Stevens played against were thugs and bad men, they saw him as an easy target, and the sad thing was, that they were right. Stevens didn't tell me who they were, or where this mysterious bar was, only that he owed them ten thousand dollars. What a goddamn idiot.

I opened my eyes and met his worried gaze. "They clearly haven't forgotten you owe them money then, eh?" I asked.

Stevens just shook his head. "They'll never forget. I'm lucky they put a rock in my window and not a bullet in my face. It's going to get worse the longer they don't have money".

"Did you pay them anything yet?". I was pretty sure I knew the answer.

Stevens was quick to respond.

"Of course not man. I don't know anyone that can make that much money in a week." He shook his head, dejected. "I'll find a way through. I always find a way.".

A moment of silence passed, I added "You know I'll help

how I can. But I have to pay rent this month and save up for a car so I don't have to walk to work every goddamn morning." Stevens looked at me, his eyes widened slightly as if he was shocked by what I said. "A car?" he asked, "Are you sure that you…" he trailed off.

I felt my blood boil. I knew why he was surprised about me getting a car, but I needed to hear him say it. "Am I sure what?". My eyes locked onto his, like the alpha wolf preparing himself for the challenge of a rival.

Stevens looked at his feet, embarrassed. "Look, man, I didn't mean anything by it. I just want to make sure that you're okay with driving again."

I quickly snapped "I am a good driver, shit just happened man. I couldn't control it."

Stevens looked taken aback. "Dude, chill out. The car was out of your control, I get that. There was ice everywhere. My concern is that you got hurt in that crash, broke both of your legs, three ribs, and thanks to the shitty installation of your airbags in your car you hit your head off the steering wheel so hard it put you into a coma for two weeks." He took a breath, calming himself. "That kind of thing is traumatic, and hard to get over. You of all people should understand"

I felt guilt in the pit of my stomach, Stevens was a good friend. He was worried about me. Sometimes my temper flared up uncontrollably, without rhyme or reason.

I breathed out and calmed down, "I'll be fine, I'm better, I'm not going back to Ha-" The walkie talkie screeched. Jackson's voice barked over the walkie "Are you two almost done? I sent you over to help Stevens over twenty minutes ago, Hank!".

I chuckled putting the walkie closer to my mouth, I could not hold back my smile. "Yeah, Jackson had to move some stuff around but we are just about to put these sheds up now."

The walkie screeched again. "It's been twenty minutes! What, you're moving the forklift with your bare hands? I swear you two drive me up the wall every day! Do you get off on my stress?"

I did good at holding back my laughter during Bill's mini tirade, but I looked at Stevens, who's cheeks were so filled with air he looked like a chipmunk with two acorns in its cheeks and he had turned beet red. At that moment I lost my cool and burst out laughing.

Stevens turned from me and hoisted himself up onto the forklift chair. Finally, time to work.

The forklift was this bulky son of a bitch that was a pain in the ass to manoeuvre around the narrow aisles. Especially seeing as the pallets needed to be hoisted up so high.

Stevens started the forklift. It beeped to life. He turned the wheel, orchestrating the movements, bending the machine to his will. He inserted the forks into the spaces and picked up the palette with ease, raising it into the air.

I looked around for a home for these sheds in the cramped shelves of the warehouse, and one space caught my eye. It was about ten feet off the ground, but it was a perfect fit.

I raised my finger, pointing to the spot.

Stevens nodded and moved the forklift over to the shelf and stretched the arms of the forklift up to the. I walked alongside the forklift to tell Stevens whether to raise or lower the forks.

"Higher!" I shouted as he moved inches away from the spot.

He raised the palette higher. It didn't seem right, still too low.

"Higher!" I shouted again. Stevens was impossibly close to the shelf. One wrong move and he damages the shelf, or could even bring everything on the shelf down on us.

The palette raised higher responding to my command.

Satisfied with the height I yelled to Stevens "Perfect, set her down!".

He put the palette down on the shelf, and he slightly lowered the forks. All he had to do was back up slowly.

Stevens yelled a cry of surprise as the forklift jerked

quickly and without control backwards. The fork dragged the pallet backwards, and the shelf, the one hundred and fifty pounds came hurdling down towards us. Towards me.

All I heard was ringing, like a hammer pounding an anvil. It got louder and louder as the box fell, until it landed on me. Then there was silence. Only silence, and that is all I remembered after that.

I awoke to a steady beeping of a heartbeat monitor. My eyes weren't open but I knew well enough what it sounded like. Each beat in my breast corresponding to the rhythmic annoying sound. I was awake but my eyes weren't open. All of the energy I had was dedicated to awakening from this haze. I didn't know how much time I had lost, how long had I spent in the fog and shadows of my own mind?

The monitor's rhythm increased as my thoughts raced a million miles an hour. What if I was blind? What if I was in a coma for twenty years? The 'what ifs?' flew through my mind like wind through the open air.

I dedicated every bit of focus on opening my eyes. I took a deep breath and let the light into my eyes, piercing through the fog of confusion.

The room I was in was white, almost everything was white. The bed I was in, the pillows where my head laid, the sheet that surrounded the perimeter of my bed, all were white.

The only bit of colour that I saw was the blue blanket that had been draped over my body.

I heard so many sounds, people calling for doctors, casual conversations of passer-by's, people running, life seemed to just be happening beyond the boundary of the curtain.

I shifted in the bed, my body responded with searing pain as if I was placed on a bonfire to burn. It suddenly occurred to me that I had no idea how I got to the hospital or what was wrong with me.

I stretched my arms straight out in front of me. It was like I had never been a human before, and was seeing how my arms worked, testing what could I do and not do with my arms and hands. When in reality I was assessing the damage. There was little pain in my arms, a few bruises on my forearms, other than that nothing of concern. Not even a broken finger.

I decided to press my luck. Slowly I raised both of my legs up. It was extremely difficult, especially with everything from the chest down being covered in a blanket. My legs didn't hurt. Thank god. I thought maybe I just was knocked unconscious, I must be fine.

I shifted to get out of this shitty bed and out of the hospital. I felt the stabbing feeling return in my chest and body. I almost screamed, the pain came so quickly and unexpectedly.

All of a sudden the curtain was thrown back, washing me

in a more intense white light.

A doctor stood in front of the bed, he wasn't even looking at me, he was looking at his clipboard with what I assumed was my information.

I stared at the doctor, a bald man with a round face and deep-set eyes. Looked almost like a supervillain. His eyes were black and soulless, devoid of life or joy. I felt a chill run through my blood like a river that never felt the heat of summer.

A moment of silence passed, with me looking at this doctor, hoping he would say anything.

The doctor let out a sigh, as if this was an inconvenience for him to be here talking to me.

He finally looked at me, I could tell immediately that I meant nothing to him, this was his job and he was only going to do it because he had to.

"Well Hank, you had an accident at work. A shed fell on you and you now have three broken ribs and a serious concussion. I'm prescribing you some painkillers, and you will be able to leave tomorrow morning. If you have any questions, ask the nurses.". The doctor then immediately placed his clipboard at the end of my bed and left.

I called out to him "Is that it?". The doctor didn't even turn his head as if he heard me, he just rushed out of the room and into the hallway.

The curtain swished again, as Stevens walked in. He was holding a plastic cup with what I presumed was water. He placed it onto the small table beside the bed.

"Hey man, I wish I could stick around to talk longer, but I have to make this quick. I just wanted to say two things. I'm sorry, the forklift, the thing just jerked so quickly, there was nothing I could do. You're lucky to be alive." Stevens took a breath and finished his last pressing point "I also wanted to warn you that your mother is coming at some point next week to check on you. Good luck buddy." He tussled my hair like I was a child and ran out of the room. I had no idea why he had to leave so soon, probably to go to a poker game or something like that. Didn't blame him either, hospitals scared the hell out of me. I spent too much time in hospitals, half the time expected to lose a limb or a piece of my mind.

I took the water that Stevens left for me. I drank a few gulps. I couldn't believe that I was that thirsty. It was like I had wandered in the desert for a day and didn't drink a drop of water the entire time. I don't know where in the hospital Stevens got this water, but I wanted some more. It was so refreshing, to such an extent that I just relaxed. Nothing could bother me now, I felt euphoric. I had just escaped a potentially lethal situation, and I was alive with a few broken bones and a concus-

 The Writers Circle 2

sion.

I chuckled and didn't stop for a while. I couldn't believe I felt this good given the circumstance.

I closed my eyes for what seemed like a moment, when I opened my eyes there the lights had all been dimmed, it must be night time.

Something felt, off. I felt someone watching me. The silence was ominous, as if there was no one alive in the hospital. As if everyone had vanished. I couldn't even hear my heart rate monitor. Something was watching me. I didn't want to look, I felt myself begin to panic. Something was coming for more, it was going to get me and steal me away into the darkest corners of the hospital.

Slowly and with great effort, I looked over my shoulder beside me. It felt like I took ages to turn my head. I didn't want to see it, I didn't want to see the terror that loomed beside me waiting to get me. I was getting slowly closer to seeing it. Closer…closer, and then I saw it was Jenna.

She sat on a chair beside me, one leg crossed over the other. She was just staring at me, smiling. I could swear, she was the reincarnation of that creepy cat from Alice in Wonderland.

"You looked so peaceful in your sleep." Jenna purred. "I heard that you were in the hospital so I thought I could come and keep you company.". The smile on her face never faltered. My heart fluttered, partially with lust, and partially with fear. I knew her being here with me wasn't good, I didn't want to be with her in the same room, or her to be near me. But I also wanted her to be near me, that was the worst part. My anxiety and fear were reaching an all-time high.

I finally found my voice, and croaked "Why can't you leave me alone?". It was blunt, but there was no point in beating around the bush.

My question never phased her, "You were never happier than you were with me. Is it so bad that I want to help you?". Her voice was as cool as ice, so calm that it enraged me.

I let my emotions take over. "You want to help me then get o—" I was cut off by the searing pain that possessed me, my ribs felt like burning stakes in my own body. My eyes squinted tightly shut, as if I didn't look at anything the pain would just go away.

Jenna stood up over me, her smile went to a look of pity. "Hank, I know we have fought, I know I hurt you. I promise I'm not here to hurt you. I want to help you, to take care of you. If not as your lover, then as a friend. If not that, then just some-one who's concerned about you.".

I looked at Jenna "I have plenty of people concerned about me, I will be just fine.". My words were so bitter I could taste it on my tongue.

She placed her hand on my shoulder, and her words cut through me like a razer. "I don't see anyone else with you, Hank. Stevens left you here, your mother borderline hates you, and the doctors, they don't care Hank. Not like I do Hank. No ones here for you like me.".

I went silent. As cruel of a point as it was, it was true.

"I'm sorry. I didn't mean for it to come off as cruel. I just want to help, that's all." Jenna whispered.

I tried to turn to my side, but the pain overtook me again. It was all I could think about.

Jenna took the water that was by me and put it to my lips. "Let me take care of you" she whispered as I drank. The pain subsided, I was able to think again.

I looked at her and nodded my head, I agreed to her helping me. I needed help. I slipped into unconsciousness again.

I left the hospital the next day. Stevens drove me home from the hospital, helped to walk me up the steps to my apartment and helped me into my bedroom and on the bed. "I told the boss man that you wouldn't be in for a while. He told me to tell you to take all the time you need, and to come to see him when you're ready." Stevens stated. "I also took the liberty of picking up your prescription for your pain medication and some water. You gonna be OK here by yourself?" He asked as he placed the water and meds on my bedside.

I nodded my head "Yeah man, thanks for doing all that. I'm in so much pain I won't be doing much aside from resting.".

I took the pill bottle, read the instructions briefly and took two of the pills. My body immediately relaxed. "You should probably go man, I'm gonna pass out really quickly. This medication is really strong." My eyes got really heavy, I felt so relaxed, as if I was suspended in air, no pressure, no pain, no worry to be had, only rest.

Darkness overtook me, and I drifted away, far away from this world and into my own mind to dream sweet and wonderful realities.

Jenna woke me up, Stevens was gone. "Hank, sweetheart. Its time to wake up." She cooed. "You need to take your medicine. She had her hand stretched out with the pill bottle in her hand. She held the salvation from my pain in her hand, such small things pills, but they had such a profound effect on the mind and body. Able to take the worst of things and make them better.

I took the pills eagerly. I didn't feel as tired as before though, I stayed awake. Jenna and I talked and laughed, just like the good old days when we were happy and together, before it all went sour.

I spent the next week in bed with Jenna by my side, she

took care of me, making sure I took my medication on time, kept me smiling and happy. She would touch my face and smile, saying she was happy when she was with me, and she wanted me always, and only me. I was always lulled to sleep by her and had the best, most refreshing sleep. Stevens also made sure to pop by every day to check on me.

I lost track of the time throughout the week. I didn't know what day it was. I awoke from a deep sleep, opening my eyes. It wasn't Jenna who woke me up this time, she was nowhere to be found. The pain was there to quickly wake me, pulsing through my body with each beat of my heart. I heard someone clearing their throat. I knew who was in my home, and the pain was the least of my worries. Footsteps approached my bedroom and the figure emerged from the living room. I looked at my mom, her hair had almost gone completely gray, her face looked permanently like she had swallowed a sour candy, and if the blue in her eyes faded any more than her eyes would go white.

"Look at yourself" she scoffed. "Have you eaten a damn thing? Do you not like taking care of yourself like a grown adult?" she pressed.

"Hello mom, I'm ok and it's great to see you too," I said sarcastically. She hadn't changed at all. Same old bitter woman.

She sneered "You were hurt at work, I came to make sure

you were still breathing and not in a ball on the floor crying for help." She walked closer towards me, I saw she had a bowl of soup. She set the bowl on my lap with a spoon in the bowl, and sat in a chair beside the bed that she must have brought into the room.

We sat in silence for what seemed like hours. I tried to think of a happier time with my mother to look back on, to make it seem like her being her wasn't so bad, that it was out of love for her son and not the obligation of a mother to come and see me. Nothing came to mind, all I felt was the dread and the burdening of me onto my mother's life.

"Well, at least this isn't like last time." Mom said casually. She continued "I was worried that you would be—". I cut her off "Crazy?" I said with venom in my voice. "No, mom. It's not like last time, there's no need to worry."

She stared at me with her icy eyes, making me feel as cold as they looked.

I looked away and ate some of my soup. I couldn't actually remember the last time I had eaten. Funny, because I also didn't remember feeling hungry in recent memory.

"No need to worry?" She asked with disbelief. Her expression changed from ice-cold, to the fury of fire erupting from a volcano.

"No need to worry." She repeated, disgusted. "Are you seeing her again?"

I felt the colour flush my face. Guilt being plastered on my pale face like a murderer being caught killing a victim. I didn't have to say anything, she knew. I attempted to deflect the question anyways. "Who?" I asked feebly.

Mom lowered in her chair, making her look like an animal ready to attack its prey, dismembering it limb from limb. I tried to not look into her eyes I was worried she would take it as a challenge

The brief still in the air was broken with mom screaming "You know fucking well who I mean! My god Hank! How pathetic are you!?". My ears were ringing from her screams. "Look what she did to our family! She destroyed us! She is not good for you! YOU PROMISED ME THAT YOU WOULD GET AWAY FROM HER! YOU BROKE YOUR PROMISE!" her eyes welled up with tears. I was so glad that Jenna wasn't here, I don't even want to think of what mom would do to her.

Mom continued her barrage of insults, slightly lower volume, but still a yell. "No one means anything to you do they? You'll go back and do anything for her, no matter the cost right?" she laughed, but I knew that laugh was just fury in a different colour.

I couldn't take anymore. "You know what mom?" I broke, tears begging to threaten to arise, the stinging warning me of their arrival.

She looked at me, her eyes widened. Basically her way of saying to bring it on.

My voice cracked "Even though Jenna hurt me, she's always been there for me. Helping, unlike you, who, when things got rough, stuck me in the Havelock ward with all the Loonies!"

I broke down and began to cry, continuing "Do you even know what they did to me? I can't even remember what I was there for! All I remember is pain!"

My body shook as I cried uncontrollably. Mom didn't move closer to console me. She didn't even show a hint of remorse. She just stared at me crying. Her voice erupted strong, with confidence.

"Let me remind you of why we put you in Havelock. Jenna and you were at your worst. You always would cry and call for her to go away. It got to the point where you said you were being tortured by Jenna. You became inconsolable and uncontrollable. At one point you tried to kill yourself to 'get away from it all'. Your dad and I had to put you in Havelock. They were the only ones who could help." She stopped staring at me and was looking off into the distance as if she was reliving it all.

"You tried to help me, eh mom? So you leave me in a room,

turn the lock and throw the key. Leaving me alone. I didn't need just a doctor, I NEEDED MY FAMILY!" I screamed uncontrollably. "What was your excuse mom? Needed to get away from your lunatic son?"

Mom immediately stood up like a viper poised to strike, moving closer until she completely loomed over me. She said "I was staying at home to help your father. He was working so much to pay for the therapists, he worked and worked. He loved you so much and just wanted you to get better." I felt tears drop on my face. Mom was crying. She continued, voice breaking as her sadness took over. "So much over time, so many hours. Each hour that he worked was a part of his life that he was giving to you, so you'd get better!"

"He didn't listen to anyone telling him to slow down. To take a day off, to get some sleep. He was in pain, but did it all for you. Up until finally the hours, the stress, the burden of you, caught up with him. His heart gave out and he died, because of you. I didn't get to say goodbye to my husband because of you."

The pain of my body didn't match the pain in my heart. My father was a good man, did what he could for whoever he could. I felt enough guilt in his death. He worked and tried to be mine and my mom's guardian angel, doing what he could to make us happy. I knew this. I always knew this.

It was time to take my medicine. I took the pill bottle.

Mom swatted the pill bottle out of my hand, knocking it to the ground.

"Sometimes pain is a necessary emotion to feel."

I just looked at her in the eyes, standing up. Even though my head was pounding, my ribs were screaming like the brakes of a train being pulled at full speed.

"Get out," I said quietly pointing out of my bedroom, and out of my apartment.

Mom's lips trembled, her eyes squinted, I saw the pain written all over her face.

She cocked her arm back and slapped me across the face hard. I saw only white as I fell to the ground to my knees. Mom had already stormed across the room and out of the apartment before I hit the floor.

I curled into myself, feeling the waves of pain, sobbing loudly.

The gentle touch of Jenna's hand on my shoulder interrupted my tears.

"Honey, I saw your mom leave. She was crying. I assume it wasn't a good visit?" Jenna said, concerned.

"You're lucky you weren't here. She would have gutted you." I said shakily.

I felt cold, so cold. As if ice were running through my

veins. I began to tremor violently.

Jenna cried "You haven't been taking your medicine. You need your medicine, love." She took a few pills out of the pill bottle on the floor.

She shoved them at me. "Take them."

I began to cry again "Maybe I deserve all this. Maybe I should just take the pain.".

"Hank! Take them!" Jenna shouted, the loudest I had ever heard her voice.

I looked up shocked. Jenna had never been that aggressive. Her face was all serious, scary, even. The look in her eyes was not right. Her glare pierced through my core.

With shaking hands, I took the pills from Jenna and swallowed them with one gulp. The familiar numbing spread through my body, all the way to my mind, dulling the painful memories that rose to the surface and threatened to overtake me.

I struggled to stand up and put myself back in bed. Laying in the fetal position saying nothing. The memories didn't go away, they didn't stop being an existing presence in my head. The memories of my father, and the guilt, wouldn't go away. Although I tried. Succeeding after taking two more pills. Eventually slipping back into sleep.

The next thing I knew, I was surrounded by darkness, with

a single beam of light shining in front of me. Jenna was in the light. I knew this was a dream. She was motionless, staring into the dark, almost like she could see through the thick blackness and see me.

"Nothing will keep us apart Hank," Jenna said. Her voice was sweet, but possessive. I didn't know why I was dreaming like this, and not of us by the pier near the water, hand in hand. Happier times. Why here, in this abyss? Something was wrong, it didn't feel right. I felt the fear well up and slowly fill up in my chest. My ears were beating like a drum to the tune of my hearts beating. I was watching Jenna's face, her eyes, go from caring and full of love, to sinister.

I heard a bone crack as Jenna contorted, her back arching forward, her head down, facing the floor. She hung there.

I struggled to find words, I couldn't think, I couldn't move, and I couldn't look away. "Je- Jenna?" I stammered.

Jenna giggled, quietly, but then loudly, so loud it seemed to fill every space of this realm. I put my hands to my ears to block out the noise. The giggling didn't seem to end. God, why didn't it end?

"You…need…me. I'm…YOURS!" Jenna shrieked. That was the last thing that I remembered. I didn't know what the hell happened next. I awoke to the morning birds cawing. I was sitting in a cold sweat. I knew one thing. That thing in my dream, that wasn't Jenna.

My heart was beating so fast, everything felt so real. I needed to keep myself grounded to reality, I looked over. Jenna was silent, looking at me worried. "Are you okay Hank?" she worried.

All I could do was nod my head. I needed to get out of my apartment. I needed to be around people. I needed to know the nightmare was over.

"I need to get out of here, I'm gonna go to the café across the street," I told Jenna. She only nodded.

I got up quickly and changed into fresh clothes and out of the pyjamas that I had been wearing for god knows how long. My ribs and my head but still hurt like hell, but mom was right about one thing, we need to feel things sometimes, no matter the pain.

I walked to the door, opening the door and walking out of the apartment. Before I left I heard Jenna ask me, "Did you take your medicine?"I nodded my head. I lied. I needed this. I needed to feel again.

I sat at the dining table with a plate of eggs and an empty cup of coffee by my side. I didn't say anything, to anyone. All I did was listen. Hearing people living their lives. Some people were having a fantastic day, bringing a joyful aura to the diner, only countered by those having a terrible day, hating every moment they were awake. Everything seemed so loud, the lights were so bright, it brought a ringing to my ears. Must be the concussion. It was funny that this was the first time I felt any effect of the concussion. My hands felt clammy and wet.

I got up and went to the washroom at the back of the diner. Dim, dirty, but that didn't matter. I went to the sink, turned the tap and let the water run cold. I slapped the water over my face, washing away sweat. A chill crept over my body as if a cold winter breeze rushed through my bones. I thought it would pass, it just got worse. I shivered and trembled uncontrollably.

Looking in the mirror above the sink, all I saw was a skull with skin stretched thin across it. The circles under my eyes were dark as the night sky. They framed bloodshot eyes, a stark contrast against my paper white skin. It didn't make sense. I had been sleeping and resting for weeks.

I bent over, trembling, to put more water on my face. Cold sweat dripped down my back.

I looked back up into the mirror and cried with surprise to see Jenna, blocking the door, a betrayed scowl on her face.

"Why did you do this?" She snarled at me.

"What do you mean?" I asked surprised.

Jenna took a step towards me. I stood in place. I was not backing down to whatever the hell this was.

     The Writers Circle 2

"You lied to me. Why did you lie?" She snapped. My face showed my bewilderment.

"I didn't lie to you…" I said hesitantly. Trying to recall how I lied to Jenna. The cold in my bones got worse, I felt the hair stand on the back of my neck. Sweat poured down my face, and my heart began to race. I could feel my anxiety growing.

"Liar!" She cried suddenly.

I jolted backward. Her cry had startled me.

"You did this! You did this to us! We could have been happy!" She shrieked. It was at that moment, Jenna grabbed her hair, and started ripping it out.

My jaw dropped in sheer terror. "Jesus, stop it, Jenna!" She kept going. Blood began to pour down from her scalp.

"JENNA STOP!" I screamed at the top of my lungs. She stopped suddenly. I saw a drop of blood trickle down into her eye, and like food colouring to water, the whites of both of her eyes changed at once to a blood red. Her pupils swallowed her irises to become deep, black pits.

I wanted to run, to get away from her. But I was trapped.

The voice that came from Jenna's lips was not hers. It couldn't be Jenna's. It sounded like an echo of a whisper from death itself. Quiet, and lethal.

"You'll never escape me. I will always be there Hank. I promise." Her face contorted to a smile, revealing a mouth of long needle-like teeth. Her ears faded until it looked like there were just empty holes in the side of her head.

With the sickening crack of breaking bones, Jenna lurched forward, her body twisted and contorted at an impossible angle.

She took a step towards me, back arched, snarling at me with those teeth.

I forgot how to breathe. I was paralyzed staring at this monstrosity coming towards me. It was going to kill me. I had to get away.

I took a deep breath and sprinted to the door. Each step took more effort than the last. The ice I felt in my bones was getting colder. I had no strength, no chance. But this was life or death. I don't know how I did it, god or some other unholy power, but I pushed through the monstrosity that was my girl-friend and escaped the bathroom.

The door burst open, I would have broken it down if I could have. I didn't stop with the door, I ran out of the café and just kept running. I was screaming, not for help, not to warn anyone about what just attacked, but because if I didn't scream bloody murder, then the terror would kill me.

I didn't run to the apartment, too easy to get me there. I let muscle memory take control. The next thing I knew, I went from running on the sidewalk, to running in the woods. I knew immediately where my legs were taking me. I was in the nature sanctuary.

My lungs heaved a last painful breath before I had to stop. I couldn't run anymore.

My head darted in every direction. The trees towered over me. Small gaps between each trunk and branch provided the perfect camouflage for me and it. The prey and the predator. I never looked behind me to see if it was behind me. If it saw where I went. I felt like it was behind me, always behind me. Letting my anxiety and terror build up until I couldn't take it. Then strike at that moment.

The only bright side was that it was daylight, and I could see through the thick of the trees.

Paranoia reached an all-time high. It had to have seen me, I thought. It must've gotten up and watched me run. It was going to sink its teeth in me and bleed me to death.

I heard a twig snap behind me. I spun around, nothing was there. My breathing got faster and faster.

I felt the air become trapped in my throat. It started to get darker. Like the sun was dying. I looked up. The sun just started dim. Until it faded to black. I couldn't see more than two feet in front of me. The night had claimed the day.

I heard the whisper in the air. "You're mine, Hank." I turned around just to see Jenna lunge at me.

I threw my fist at her so hard I thought my hand would shatter. It missed completely.

"You can't fight me, Hank." It hissed.

We circled each other like animals in a deathmatch. The air felt like a blizzard, and sweat trickled into my eyes as if I had them under a faucet.

Jenna stopped, looked at me with those horrid eyes. Winking at me, like this was a child's game, and uttered "Gotcha,' with her nightmare smile.

I stood confused for a millisecond. That was when I felt the electricity course through my body, and I fell to the ground.

Yet again, I woke up in a hospital bed. This time I was restrained with my arms and legs bound to the bed. Panic set in immediately as I thrashed trying to move my arms and legs to free myself. I was a trapped, frightened animal stuck in a cage.

Wide-eyed in fear, I searched the room. That thing must be here. I didn't know where, but I could feel it. The cold was still in the very core of my bones, the sweat was still running down my face. That had to be its calling card when it was near. That was the only thing that made sense.

I began screaming. I needed help, someone needed to free me, to save me.

I saw a doctor come in. He looked very calm.

I could tell he was different, he looked like he cared. He

was even looking me in the eyes like a human being and not a part of his job.

The doctor stood at the edge of my bed, I could see his face more clearly. The white hair and beard, and his blue eyes calmed me. His friendly face told me that no harm would come to me. His face looked familiar. That is when it dawned on me. I was back in Havelock. This was the psychiatrist.

"Hello, Hank. I'm not sure if you remember me, but my name is Nick. I'm sorry to see you back here."Nick spoke softly, as if a decibel louder would break me.

I wasted no time, as ludicrous as it would sound. "Nick, you gotta listen, it's Jenna, she-"

Nick interrupted me. "So Jenna is back," he sighed, moving closer to me.

"Hank you've had a hard life, and I am so sorry. We tried so hard and it seemed like we had gotten rid of her. But, seems like you were tempted once again."

I erupted "Nick this isn't about a fucking spurned lover! She turned into a monster! She just snapped and turned into a monster! Therapy doesn't cure monsters!" I knew that I sounded like someone out of a movie, trying to claim that it was real. "Also how is this my fault!? How did I tempt this thing?" I cried.

Nick pulled up a chair beside the bed and took a deep

breath. "Hank, why didn't you pick up your painkillers?"

I was shocked. I just told him that a monster tried to kill me, and he's worried about my medication.

"NICK! I got my medication! Stevens picked it up for me!" I was even more bewildered than before. If that was even possible.

As soon as I said that, a police officer walked into the room, didn't say a word, just produced a picture of Stevens.

"Why are you showing me a picture of Stevens?" I asked.

The officer responded solemnly. "Sir, this man you call Stevens, he's been seen dealing drugs for a gang we have been monitoring for a while. It's our belief that he has been dealing to you for a while."

My mouth dropped with anger. "I got my medication prescribed by a hospital here, Stevens got it for me. I don't do drugs recreationally. I had to take these painkillers because of my accident."

Nick spoke out "Hank we ran a blood test and took a urine sample. We found large quantities of a street drug people are calling 'Cloud', its an opioid. Very potent and long-lasting."

The officer added on, "Stevens may have been giving you this drug to test it, or to make you a customer. Did he have money problems?"

I didn't even have time to think about it before my head

began nodding yes. "He lost a lot of money in a poker game apparently," I stated with dread.

"He was probably selling this drug as part of his debt then, you were going to be his next customer." The officer looked at me with sympathy.

"I'm sorry, son." He walked away from me, then added, "We will be checking your statements, you'll be hearing from us again.". He then faded away into the hallway.

I let everything sit for a moment, Stevens betrayed me. No wonder he checked on me so often for the first while, he wanted to make sure that his new customer didn't overdose on his product.

Nick broke the brief silence "Hank, do you remember when you were last admitted to Havelock?".

I looked at him and shook my head, that time was all a blur.

"You said that Jenna was abusing you, that she was hurting you. This was after your car accident."

"What are you trying to get at Nick?"

Nick looked down at his shoes, "Jenna's not real, Hank.".

I laughed. "Of course she's real, she was taking care of me. She-"

Nick cut me off again. "Made sure you took your medicine?"

I recoiled in horror. How did he know what she did?

"Yeah, she did that last time too. The truth is Hank, last time you were here, it wasn't because of your injuries, or this fictional character Jenna. You were abusing your painkillers, this 'Jenna', always got mad when you didn't take your painkillers. So you always took them. More and more, until she never stopped hurting you. This is your craving. Hank Jenna is your craving for the painkillers, from the escape it gave you from feeling, and Hank, your craving is a cold cruel bitch. She would always tell you to take your medicine at the beginning of withdrawal. This new drug you took, that Stevens allegedly slipped to you, it worsened your craving. It made Jenna a monster."

Nick paused for a moment "Your mom, all of us, we pretended she was real because we thought it would be less traumatic to you. We used hypnotherapy, and even shock therapy to try to repress your memories. We didn't know she would come back." He continued.

I looked at Nick in awe. Everything, my reality seemed to unravel like yarn. The truth just destroyed everything I knew or thought was real. "She's real, she has to be." I stammered in a feeble attempt to grab a hold back on reality. "What about what happened in the woods? Jenna, the monster, it was there!"

Nick was still looking at the floor, shaking his head. "Witnesses saw you in the woods. You were darting around for hours until an officer approached you. You threw a punch at him, you guys circled each other until the policeman's partner tazed you. Brought you here. You hallucinated during your withdrawal, that's when this monster appeared."

Tears formed in my eyes, I nodded my head. That's what Jenna meant when she screamed at me for lying. I didn't take my medicine. Symptoms were showing, the paranoia, anxiety, sweating like I had a fever, and cold to the bone.

I began to cry. My head was down, defeated. Tears poured down my face, "I don't know what's real anymore." I sputtered.

Nick looked up at me and clasped my hand. "Hank, this is real. Your battle with addiction is real, I am real, and you are real." He paused. "Jenna is a figment of a very real battle. When you use, she will make you feel like the happiest man in the world. When you don't use, that's when your nightmare comes to life. But that is when you have the power, that's when you can fight this. Don't let her win Hank, don't give her what she wants."

I looked at Nick "I thought she wasn't real?" I asked. My mind ready to have its world flipped again.

"She's not real to us. But she is very real for you. She's your demon that your fighting. I'll be there to help you fight her. But it is your battle. We all have our demons, Hank. But we all have the power to give up, or be victorious." Nick then pulled out a coin from his pocket. "I know what you're going through. This is a twelve-year sober chip. I am going to help you win this. But you have you be the one to decide to win."

I looked at Nick in the eyes and just nodded my head. "Help me win this then, Nick," I said quietly.

He smiled. "Get some rest, tomorrow you will begin rehabilitation therapy. There are still some of the drugs in your system that need to be metabolized and excreted. See you tomorrow Hank."With that, Nick disappeared into the hallway.

I sat back in the bed, just processing what I had heard. A nurse walked in.

"Nurse I'm sorry, I don't mean to be rude, but can I please just have a second alone?" I asked politely.

Her back was turned to me. She didn't say anything.

"Nurse?" I repeated, my heart began to beat.

"You will never get rid of me Hank. I'll always be with you." The nurse whispered.

My blood ran cold as the nurse turned to face me. The needle-like teeth, the red and black eyes. "You and I get some quality time now Hank!" The monster giggled.

My screams rang out throughout the hospital hallways for

days to come.

PERIPHERAL
HOLDEN PRIMEAU

Just another security gig.

I arrived about twenty minutes early for my interview. It was with a guy named Arnold, some hotshot manager that talked like he was king shit. There are so many of these ass hats running security teams these days.

When I entered the lobby, you could tell it was recently renovated to give the ancient building that polished turd look. You can polish shit all you want, but in the end, it's still crap. Even if you splurged on the fancy gift wrap.

As I approached the front desk, a portly woman was behind it. She had on a bright pink blouse and covered her eyes with black owl rimmed glasses.

"Excuse me, I am here for the night watchmen position; my interview is with Arnold at two this afternoon. Could you let him know I have arrived?"

"Certainly, sir. You are quite early, so the chances are you will have to wait a little bit. Is that alright?"

I nodded and made my way to the new lobby chair. They still smelt like they were in an IKEA showroom. I sat for about half an hour before this young-looking guy with a Clark Kent jaw came walking up to me. He had a smile that could convince the devil to surrender hell.

He reached out his right hand, "Arnold Walters." Then he ushered me up to an interview room.

After a painfully dull interview, I found out that I got the job. I was to start out at thirteen and some change per hour, but I got the chance of an increase in 6 months. Bullshit if you ask me, but I needed the money.

I got a short tour of the building from Arnold, an introduction to the building manager, and the creepiest of grins from both of them. They looked like the goddamn Cheshire Cat.

***

Moist, why does it always seem that the air gets fucking moist? Sticking to the insides of your nostrils clawing up your lungs with each shortened breath.

I strode my way into the building hitting the card access reader on the way in. My card reader was on a retractable lanyard that made this *SSSLLLRRRAAAPPPTTT* sound as it went back into its rested position.

I sauntered my way down the dimly lit hallway toward the Security office. I waved to Jeff, one of the overnight cleaners on my way in. I hit the card reader again, *SSSLLLR-RRAAAPPPTTT*.

I walked in about half an hour early to relieve the day guard. He just had a small child, and they made his position a hybrid with health and safety responsibilities. I walked in and saw the exhaustion in his eyes. The dark circles reminding me of some distant planet's outer rings.

"Hey, Dave, what's going on?"

He slowly looked up from the display to meet my eyes, "Jesus you're early. You gotta get a life, Greg."

I chuckled to humour him, but told him it's time to go home. Without any argument, Dave got up from the seat gave me a debrief. "The only thing you've gotta worry about tonight is Jeff. The guy is bound to snap someday."

My laugh is genuine this time, and I slapped him on the shoulder with the back of my hand before he was on his way out of the building. I watched my displays to make sure he got clocked out.

I threw on the cameras and saw the cleaners do their routine, the poor bastards trying to finish all the cleaning by midnight. I go for two security patrols at this time. The night felt long.

***

I shook myself awake and wiped the trickle of drool from my chin. It's a quarter past one in the morning. I was due for a security patrol fifteen minutes before I woke up. I got out of my seat in the office and washed my face with cold water from the sink. I tried to shake the tired and wash the sleep from my eyes. I was on day six of a seven-day work stretch, and I just needed to pull through these last two nights. I felt like I do more sleeping than anything else with this job.

I got up and scanned the door, *SLLLLRRRRAAAPPPPTTT*, walked out of the office and turned down the right hallway to start the walk. A feeling of panic crept up my chest as I walked through the shipping and receiving area. I tried to shake it off, but it clung to me. It was almost as if the air itself was corrupted with this feeling. The further I walked, the deeper I sank down into it, its claws digging into me.

I rounded the corner to the boiler room, and it was really bright. Damn boilers gave off so much light and the heat was something else entirely. The air got sticky. Damp and overpowering as I went into the room. I almost turned around to exit, but I saw something moving behind the furthest boiler out of the corner of my eye. For a moment, I thought that it must be a cleaner and tried to shake the rising feeling of panic.

Then I remembered that before my walk, I did a system search to see if there were some cleaners still in the building. There wasn't supposed to be anyone left.

I grabbed my flashlight and shone it on the area. Nothing but a pile of rags and an old jumpsuit. I exhaled until my belly stretched my belt and the pinching of my hairs reminded me to inhale. New job jitters. Ain't nobody fucking here.

I reached the second floor of the building and felt foolish for being so freaked out. All things considered, I've been doing this shit for over fifteen years. Some creepy room shouldn't even phase me anymore.

As I got to the top of the stairs, I heard a scraping on the floors behind me. I tried my best not to think about it, but reflex and instinct got the better of me. As I began to turn my head, I saw that something was following me. It was walking on three of its four legs, dragging one behind it. There was a trail of aquamarine coloured liquid on the floor. Its skin was beige and so tightly stretched against its organs and muscles that it looked like drying leather. Its eye sockets seemed to be hollow, but as I saw them more clearly, the creature's opaque, purple eyes just looked like they had sunk into its skull. I stared at the thing, it traced my face with its look in return.

I wanted to scream, but all I could manage to do was back up and trip over the last step. I scrambled to grab my flashlight and use it as some sort of make-shift baton. Falling hard onto my back, I struggled to move, and my eyesight got a little hazy. I turned the light on and shook it in the monster's direction until my vision came back.

It was gone. I should have been staring straight at it, but it had vanished. I slowly crawled away from the stairs until I felt my back bump into a door. I got to my feet and grabbed the handle, flinging it open and slamming it shut behind me. Out of the corner of my eye, I saw the creature again. It slammed its body against the door so hard the glass window cracked, and the frame contorted inward.

***

My first thought was, "Fuck this."

"What the fuck is this thing?" was the second.

I had to think about how I was getting back to the office. Better yet, how was I going to get out of the building. Sprinting down the hallway, I threw open the doors to the main level. There were three scan doors to make it through until I got to the office, five until I was outside of my car, and then I could get the fuck out of there. I was at the first door in about thirty seconds flat. I hit the scanner control and the lock slapped open before a satisfying *SSSLLLRRRAAAPPPTTT*. I similarly tore through the next door. I was running down the long hallway before I tripped over what felt like nothing. I felt a warmth creep onto my legs before they felt limp.

I didn't want to look. When I did, I saw my legs being swallowed by the creature like I was on a conveyor belt. Its jaws unhinged as the thing was looking directly into my eyes. Numbness spread across my body and at that moment I felt I couldn't do anything to prevent my fate. The pain was immeasurable. I felt my skin break under the pressure of its jaws closing, and my blood spilling into its mouth. As it dragged me in, toward the back of its throat, it kept its stare. Never faltering as it consumed me.

I decided it was time to act before it was too late. I swung my flashlight as hard as I could behind me. Through my peripheral vision, I realized that I hit the thing right in its fucking eye. A sickeningly loud pop went off in my ear and some foul black ooze poured from the creature's eye socket. It let out a wail that sounded like wind making its way through the gaps in rocks on an ocean shore. Soon after, it released me from its jaws. Without waiting to reason with my injuries, I got up and slammed my card down on the second card reader. It lit up green, and the familiar *SSSLLLRRRAAAPPPTTT* went off.

I pushed through the door and slammed it behind me. Its locks shut and I began to run towards the final door in my path until the office. Metal doors crashed behind me as I went flying down the hallway. I don't look this time to see it, I already know what it is. I gave the last of my energy to sprint to the last door and slam my card onto the reader. It flashed red... Fuck, it was a code door. I hit my card again and typed in my password. It goes red again... Fuck, how did these things work, again? I hear the sound of the metal doors scraping on the ground behind me. The fucking thing was right behind me, dragging pieces of the hallway with it. I entered my code, then swiped my card. Green. The fucking thing turned green. I let go of my card and heard *SSSLLLRRRAAAPPPTTT*.

I tore the fucking door open and slammed it behind me. I took the fire axe from the wall and put it between the handles in an attempt to secure the door more. I ran full tilt to the security office door. I slammed my card on the reader, and it turned green. I jumped through the entrance, landed on my back, and turned to kick the door shut.

When I looked down at my legs to assess the damage done to them, I saw deep gouges on each side of both legs. The tissue appeared to have been pierced by dozens of tiny teeth. It seemed as if the blood and muscle had been sucked out. I looked for my first aid kit so that I could cover my legs in antibacterial liquids. It hurt. Bad. After it was clean, I covered it in gauze and medical tape.

I just needed to make it until 7 AM. That's when the lights would come on and I wouldn't be alone anymore. Just gotta wait till sunup... Yeah, just gotta wait...

***

My eyes slowly began to fill with colour. As my vision came back, everything looked like I was peering through waxed paper. I started to push myself up, and I heard alarms going off on the control panels. I was able to pull myself up to the console and saw that multiple doors were forced open all over the complex. It all started in the science division.

I checked the time of the first breach. It was shortly after 1:15 AM. That's right around the time I started my walk, no wonder I missed it. I pulled up security footage of the area in question and saw the entire containment chamber of the science area. Chamber One Alpha is what the label said.

The door on the chamber exploded outwards before that thing that tried to eat me crawled out over the glass. Its back leg got snagged on a larger shard and its aquamarine blood began to gush out. From there, it smashed through multiple doors until I could see it headed towards the boiler room. Shortly after this, I saw myself slowly walking from the other direction. Fuck sakes. If I had headed from the other way first, I would have been tipped off. Of course, typical fucking Greg.

I made a mouth out of my right hand and moved it as I spoke, "Oh no. I can't go that way first, that's the end of the walk."

Fucking routines. Hindsight, and all that.

I grabbed my keys, coat, and a duffel bag filled with my lunch and supplies. I checked the time on the office clock. It was 6:45 AM. Time for me to get the hell out of there and seal this building.

I looked at the console and began to enter the lockdown procedure. I cycled through the cameras in an attempt to locate the thing, but I wasn't having any luck. I was tempted to abandon the search, but I caught a glimpse of it in the cafeteria. It was ripping through the food storage.

Figuring that I had enough distance between me and it, I entered the command for the lockdown procedure. Deafening alarms blared throughout the facility.

A robotic voice boomed through every room, hallway, and stairwell, "Emergency lockdown procedure commenced. You have 15 minutes until automatic shutters seal the building. Emergency override expires in 10 minutes."

***

I shuffled down the corridor as I kept a close eye on the cameras with my security tablet. I needed to keep an eye on that thing. It was still in the food stores, unaffected by all the noise going on around it. I slowly crept around a corner and kept an eye out for my exit. Flashing amber lights went off all around me, and emergency strobe flashers were going off at the same time. I looked back at the tablet to check in on the creep. The thing stopped eating and was staring right at the camera. It was inches away from it. It felt like it was staring straight at me. I froze, staring straight back at it. It tore out of the room, letting out that wail... I could hear it. Even from across the facility.

I grabbed my emergency keys and put them into a key slot behind me. As I twisted the key, automated shutters, the kind that looked like they were ripped out of a mall, slid down from the ceiling. I was trying to seal off the hallway. Hearing the locks click in place was almost as satisfying as a plate of shawarma. I doubted it would stop it, but it would buy me enough time to get away from it.

As I reached the last two sets of double doors, I decided it was time to seal off the rest of the hallways behind me. I entered a command to track all cameras that detect motion. Anywhere that thing went, I wanted to know about it. The command finished processing and two cameras were revealed to be picking up movement. One was focused on me pacing, but the second feed was from a camera very close to me. It was past all the barriers I had already sealed. The thing was closing in fast. The second feed was switching within seconds. Fuck it... I approached an override keyhole, entered my key, and turned it to the right twice, listening for the clicks.

The robotic voice boomed a second time, "Emergency lockdown procedure commenced. You have 5 minutes until automatic shutters seal the building. Emergency override has expired."

I sprinted to the exit as fast as I could. I kept the tablet's screen in the corner of my eye, taking peeks at that thing. It was moving even faster. It's like it knew what I was trying to do. I went through three sets of double doors, slamming them behind me as I went. Frozen in place, I saw that damn exit clear as day, but the camera showed that thing in my path. I could have sworn that nothing was there.

I turned my head sideways and I could see the thing in my peripheral vision. It stood on its back legs, one still leaking that aquamarine coloured blood. It stared at me with its remaining purple eye, where the left one used to be was an empty socket, leaking black sludge. I knew there was no turning back at this point. It was time for me to try and get out by all means necessary.

I sprinted right at it like I was a damn rhino charging at a threat. I dove underneath its belly right after I chucked my bag above its head. Damn, that felt cool. Using my peripheral vision, I watched as it attacked the bag headed straight for its face. I made it through the door and slammed it shut behind me. I made sure every lock was secured and the door was reinforced with anything that I could find. The damn thing couldn't stop me now.

As I ran down the stairs, I could hear it bending the door that I had sealed. Its wails escaped through these bends. I rounded the corner and saw that the exit was only about ten meters away. I reached for my retractable key card and slapped it against the card reader. It ignited green and that amazing *SSSLLLRRRAAAPPPTTT* was music to my ears. I dove outside as fast as I could. The door slammed shut and the tone played out again.

BEEPUURN! BEEPUURN! The robotic voice boomed throughout the building one last time, "Emergency lockdown commencing. Please stand clear of the emergency gates."

Steel shutters slid over the exit and I heard the locks slide into place. I finally got some time to breathe as I walked toward my 2008 Chevrolet Impala. I unlocked the door, slid in, and began to sit down in the driver's seat. As I adjusted my rear-view mirror, I noticed a blinking coming from the tablet.

Everything in me told me to ignore it, but I had to see what it said.

My mouth went barren and a cold sweat crept over my skin. The alert was for a failed barrier seal. That means that thing could have made it out. I frantically adjusted my rear-view mirror, trying to get a glimpse of it. Feeling uneasy, I went to reach for the door handle, but something pierced my back and burst through my chest.

I looked down to see my chest ripped open and blood pooling at my feet. There was nothing there, just a giant hole and too much blood. I turned my head to the side and peered out of the corner of my eye. Teeth. Rows of them surrounding a long, spiralling tongue. The creature recoiled from me and I fell forward. I tried my best to look up at the thing sitting in my back seat.

My vision slowly faded, as I felt it drinking me up. I looked at it, and its damaged eye slowly seemed to regenerate. Now, both purple eyes looked at me, and an amber glow appeared deep within them. It retracted its tongue into its mouth, and a smile spread across its face.

Letting out a whisper of a laugh, it spoke to me. "You were the best of them yet. The tastiest treat. I can't wait to meet the next Security Guard that sits in your seat."

RISE OF YBON
LOGAN PRIMEAU

Chapter 1

A young elf lay face down on the ground in a grove of trees that was recently set alight, his blood pooling underneath him. The acrid smoke that filled the air caused him to cough uncontrollably. Dens Ka'fell was a Keeper, one of the specially trained stewards of the Elven Forests. At his feet sat a shattered sword, the source of his grievous wounds. The hilt bore the seal of Kalraxix, the Bandit King.

It had been ten years since the armies of Kalraxix had first begun their conquest of the elven towns dotting the coast and those in the eastern lands. Never had an army come this far north, into the lands surrounding Yul Es. The land here had long ago been settled by the elves of Fell to the west. Life here was simple and fair. Large groves of Elven Trees surrounded small farming villages. The rich soil provided the elves here

with enough nutritious food that they were able to export sur-
pluses to the capital in the west. It was because of this that the
elves here were able to enjoy one of the highest standards of
living in the empire.

As Drens lay there feeling the life drain from him he began
to hear what sounded like whispers in the distance. It was as if
1000 voices were trying to speak all at once and he strained to
hear them. With all of the energy he had left in his failing body,
Drens pulled himself towards one of the many trees surrounding him that were not yet set ablaze. His right arm had gone
limp so with his left arm he pulled himself along the ground
slowly. As he approached the tree, he was able to spot an exposed root. Pulling himself up against the trunk of the tree he
pulled off a silken glove from his right hand and pressed it
against the exposed root. Several hyphae began to emerge
from his hand, penetrating the root below. It was then Drens
was hit with the full force of the voices which had just been
whispers before. The voices were screaming in tremendous
pain overwhelming his senses. He was able to tap into his
training as a Keeper and focus his mind on blocking out the
screams.

Once connected to the Saa, the High Elven uni-mind, he
was able to call for help, "Hear me, Lord, I need your help", he
pleaded weakly. Surely the Lord of the Elven People Eleywa

would be able to help. He hoped the screams that overwhelmed his senses previously would not drown out his pleas for help. The devastation going on must have been too much as he did not receive a reply. As more blood seeped from his body Drens became very weak, unable to even hold up his head anymore he slumped to the ground once more. He lay there with his head on the ground in silence as he felt himself fading away. At this point, he accepted his fate. This was his time to go and he felt an overwhelming sense of peace as he felt his body succumb to the cold and begin to shut down. As he let go of his focus blocking out the screams of the Saa he spoke his final words to all of those connected. "I love you all", he said his eyes welling up with tears, "I look forward to joining you in eternity." With his last words spoken and a smile on his face, he closed his eyes and waited for the rest of his life to leave his body.

In his mind's eye, a figure of light appeared, blinding at first. As the light faded a familiar face formed before him. "Mother?" he asked eagerly tears now streaming from his eyes.

"My son," the figure said in a soothing melodic voice. The figure placed a hand on Drens shoulder and continued. "You have been gravely injured."

"Yes, mother I was attacked by bandits from the south. I attempted to stop them from burning the groves but was unsuccessful. Now I am fated to join my ancestors in the Saa ear-lier than I had anticipated," he said a wry smile washing over his face.

"You will not be joining us today," his mother reassured him, "I will not allow my son to join me if I can help it."

"No, you cannot! You wouldn't survive the process and I can't lose you again," he pleaded, his eyes tearing up once again. "Please!"

"My beautiful son always worrying about others before himself. I miss you with all that I am. I hope you can forgive me for this," she stated as the light surrounding her grew intensely bathing the entire area in light blinding Drens momentarily. Hyphae began to grow from the roots of the tree and enter through the holes left in Drens chest by the bandit's sword. The wounds came together and bound within moments stopping the ooze of blood. Throughout his body, a comforting warmth grew. A brilliant glow surrounded his slumped body illumi-nating the trees surrounding him. Ghostly forms of light stood in a circle as if watching over him at the edge of the clearing. Their murmurs were now audible over the low hum of the magic at work inside Drens.

Suddenly the writing stopped and in an instant, Drens shot up with a deep breath and opened his eyes. The hyphae retreated back into the root system of the tree and Drens rose to his feet, whole again. When running his hands over the areas he was stabbed the skin had grown back and the bones underneath were mended. It felt as though he had never been injured and there was still a warm glow to his skin that was radiating heat. As he stood there in awe, he could faintly hear the voice of his mother fading away. "I love you, son," she said and then she was gone. She had sacrificed herself and her life energy so that he should live on. It had been six years since his mother had died, and this was the only time he had spoken to her since. Now she was gone, and he still had to face the terrible situation he found himself in. Overwhelmed with guilt and sorrow Drens falls to his knees and begins to sob uncontrollably. The forest around him is filled with the faint screams of thousands of souls and the dull roar of an encroaching forest fire.

Chapter 2

Lord Ciaran Carswell sits stiffly in a chair by the fire. Gazing into the flames his thoughts focussed on the deeds that stood before him. He had been named Lord over ten years ago and was just now consolidating the armies of men under one banner. For too long humans had suffered under the thumb of the Elven Empire of the far west. Nearly half of their harvest was given up in tribute every year to their elven masters. Refusal to do so was met with swift and brutal punishment. Now with the Civil War raging in the southwest along the coast Fell had demanded that Lord Carswell and his counterparts supply soldiers to fight the Bandit King and his followers. Their losses had been great. Thousands of men and women who marched off to fight in a war that was not of their own making never returned to their families in the east. Instead, they lie dead in shallow mass graves that dotted the coastal lands. This had fueled contempt amongst the humans, and it came to a head with the defeat of Imperial forces at Sa'Va. The bandits were now veritably on the doorstep of the realm of humans and this made many nervous. In all of its attempts to protect the people east of Yuleywa, the Empire had failed. If humans were going to survive, they would need to put aside their intergroup conflicts and unite as one people. Lord Carswell had finally succeeded in doing so and was able to muster a force of twenty thousand fighting men and women ready to defend the realm from external forces.

At this very moment, that army was camped just south of Yuleywa, known as Lake Eleywa in human language. For now, they were a deterrent force keeping stray raiders and brigands from entering human lands from the south. Carswell knew though that his force would not go unnoticed for long and that eventually, they would need to fulfill their intended purpose.

This was to be Lord Carswell's invasionary army, a wedge to drive into the heart of elven territory and ensure human autonomy from the rest of the Empire. If Lord Carswell was successful in his plan humans would finally be able to pry themselves from under the control of the elves who basically held them captive in their own lands. Failure would mean almost certain annihilation.

The weight of it all caused Lord Carswell to sigh deeply and take a sip of the fine Hordrec wine that filled his chalice. The other Lords of the realm thought him mad. They were content in living out their meek existence paying homage to an absentee master thousands of miles away in Fell. They felt humans were too weak to fight off the Empire and elves in their current state. They had seen whole villages razed for much less than the treason that Carswell proposed. Fear kept them rooted in the status quo. Carswell knew better than they the power humans were able to wield. Humans had come a long way from the primitive peoples that first come to the eastern coasts by canoe from the Islands. Contact with the dwarves of the Serpentine Mountains had granted them access to stronger ores and more valuable gems. The discovery of Faeries allowed for faster communication over larger distances than ever before. Humans were even able to now wield low magics through extensive study and the use of alchemy.

There was even hope in the war that raged between the Empire and the Bandit King Kalraxix. With the Empire focussed on their new enemy they had less time to ensure that their human subjects were falling in line which allowed for much more autonomy than they had ever enjoyed before. Scouts from the west had even reported that many groves of Elven Trees in the area surrounding the sacred Yul Es were burning or completely destroyed by the encroaching armies of Kalraxix. Known as Mwelpra in the elven tongue these trees were sacred to High Elves as they were not only the remains of their ancestors but also an astral network of sorts. Powered by the magic of their god Eleywa these groves were like a hive mind that contained all of the collective souls of the elven dead. Losing them was a great spiritual defeat to the elves and this was something that Carswell understood very well that the other Lords did not. In his view, the Empire was caught in a time of great chaos and if humans were going to claim their independence then this was the time to do it.

Carswell took another nervous sip from his cup before setting it down and moving to his bedroom. He stood in the doorway staring at his wife asleep in their bed. Their two young children also lay fast asleep at her side impervious to the stress that surrounded them. It was for them that Lord Carswell was staking everything he had. So that they could enjoy a life of freedom, a life that he had been robbed of. With a swift motion, he downed the rest of his wine and moved quickly towards the stables near the rear of the hold. If he was going to make it to the army by daybreak he would need to leave now. In the stables his personal guard awaited. Ten of the finest warriors of the realm stood ready for his command. Without saying a word Lord Carswell donned his helmet and mounted his horse. Amruless, a sleek all-white stallion already loaded with provisions to last the journey then slowly made its way towards the exit of the stables. Without a word, Carswell nodded to the stable keeper who threw open the door and Carswell rode out swiftly his personal guard following closely behind.

The echo of horses' hooves filled the night air as they followed the roads leading northwest towards Lake Eleywa. The sun was only beginning to rise, and the grasslands were covered in a thick blanket of dew. The destination was Fort Nordhaas a few hours ride away. There Carswell would be able to meet up with the bulk of his army and lay his plans to move further west.

Chapter 3

Smoke filled the air in the grove that surrounded Drens causing him to begin coughing. This forced him to come to his senses and deal with the situation unfolding around him. With the fires engulfing all of the trees in the area Drens had no choice but to leave. There would be no way to save any of them and this realization caused an anxious pang in his chest. Nearly a thousand years of history was being destroyed before him. On the ground near where he had fallen was the broken sword which was now useless and a small buckler. Besides a crack in part of the wood, it was intact.

Drens picked it up quickly and searched around the area some more. On the ground, ten yards away was a small dagger which must have fallen in the struggle that had left him fatally wounded. Moving swiftly Drens picked it up stashed it in his belt and moved on. For some reason, he felt lighter as if he was not moving across the ground but floating. Scanning the horizon Drens was able to see an area of the forest still unaffected by the fire and made his way towards it. As he approached the edge of the forested area, he noticed more bodies littering the forest floor. They were Keepers like himself, more victims of the savage bandits. After quickly searching for any signs of life Drens kept moving towards the edge of the forest as quickly as possible. Once making it to clearing on the eastern edge of the forest Drens took a moment to rest and contemplate his next move. Southward in the distance, he could see more flames, these ones coming from a set of torches. Accompanying the playful flames of the torches were the sounds of several men laughing and celebrating merrily. Stealthily Drens made his way towards the source of the sounds. Once at the edge of their camp Drens stopped and hid behind some shrubs.

"Ai did you see the look on that tall one's face," one of the bandits said with delight, "nothing better than watching the life drain from their eyes I say!"

A raucous cheer erupted from the group as they lifted mugs filled with ale up into the air. There were four of them clad in makeshift armour, armed with elven long swords and bucklers similar to the one Drens had picked up from the grove. Taking on four well-armed enemies was nothing short of suicide but Drens was not thinking of that. In fact, he could not think, all he could feel was a white-hot rage filling him inside. His hand clutched at the dagger he had picked up while fleeing the grove and he removed it from his waistband. With the dagger held tightly in hand and the buckler in the other Drens silently moved on the group. None of the bandits noticed him as he snuck up behind the one that had bragged about his kill.

Without much thought behind it, Drens leapt up behind the burly elf and drove the dagger downwards into the space between his collar bone and throat. A quick twist of the dagger opened his neck up and was followed by an explosion of blood.

The rest of the bandits scrambled to face the attacker pulling out their swords and readying themselves. The wounded bandit fell to his knees clutching at his neck and Drens stepped over him to face the rest of the group. Drens used the buckler to deflect an incoming blow from one of the attacker's swords and then followed it up with a thrust of the dagger. It hit its mark and entered into the bandit's chest via a weak spot in his plate armour. Almost as if by reflex Drens kicked the bandit in the chest which released the dagger. As he turned to face the rest of the soldiers, he was able to deflect a blow from another of their swords. The momentary imbalance this created allowed Drens to drive his dagger deep into the elf's upper chest. Drens removed the blade with a twist and the elf fell to his knees clutching his hemorrhaging chest.

With the bandits dead, Drens fell to his knees and began to weep. His body tingled with the power that now coursed through his veins. He took a moment to reflect but then made his way to his feet. He checked the bandit's bodies for anything useful and found a scroll on one of them which had some plans drawn up. It showed that the Bandit King was moving a large contingent of units north to Twill'Bru to siege the city and take it into his fold. There were detailed battle plans, unit sizes, names of generals and more. This could be the only chance that Drens would get to one-up the Bandit King and exact revenge for the death of his family. Drens had to make it to Twill'Bru before the armies of the Bandit King so he could warn them and help organize a counter-attack. Local governments were known to be corrupt but Drens thought they should still listen, so he started to make his way north. He found now that he had increased stamina and so he began to run at full speed, something he was now able to sustain indefinitely.

With his now increased speed Drens made it to the edge of Twill'Bru in less than an hour. He made his way to the town hall where he was able to get an audience with the mayor. The mayor was an elf named Garswick that wore human fashions and spoke elvish with an accent.

"I was ambushed south of here near a bandit encampment and I found a scroll that you should be made aware of," Drens explained to the mayor. He handed the parchment over and the mayor read it over.

"This is exactly what we don't need right now," the mayor exclaimed and slammed his fist down on his desk. "Those bandits are really a pain in the you-know-where kid," he huffed. He began to file through his desk now looking for something.

"I want to help," Drens blurted out as the mayor shuffled through his things. This caused the mayor to stop and look at him.

"Look kid we got professionals that care of this sort of

stuff. Here why don't you take this and head down to the Dro'Ik Inn they have great ale," the mayor said as he handed Drens a handful of gold coins. "Trust me, we got this. I just need to find this damn signal stone so that I can make contact with the capital."

Drens just got up and quietly left as the mayor continued to rifle through his desk. He had been blown off and just made his way in a daze to the pub that the mayor had mentioned.

Chapter 4

Far below the surface of the Serpentine Mountains lay ornately carved caverns. Home to the dwarves, Lalhaal is a gigantic underground metropolis. Hustle and bustle fill the streets as people go on about their day. The air is filled with the sound of merchants and the smell of roasted meat. The walls of their city are meticulously carved with reliefs inset with precious stones. Most doorways and windows are lined with gold and the people wear fine silk clothing. Below the streets lay the heart of the Glimmermine, a large deposit of lodestone a type of magically infused rock. Mining lodestone had proven lucrative for the dwarves.

A young dwarf named Beocarn had just begun his new job in the mine and was going about his daily routine. His job was to pick up the slag left behind when a crew was finished with an area. Today was like any other day and Beocarn found himself deep within the mine making his way towards the freshest tunnels. The walls here hummed with energy radiating off the lodestone and the tunnel walls glowed faintly purple-red.

For a few months, the dwarves had noticed the lodestone becoming more and more potent. The stone they found in the deepest parts of the mine had magical properties much stronger than normal. Section 4F was the freshest of these tunnels and where Beocarn had found himself assigned today.

As he made his way through the tunnel towards the end, he noticed the area was unusually quiet. Normally the tunnels were filled with the sounds of working dwarves. There would normally be the sounds of metal tools ringing out against rock and boisterous laughter. Today the tunnels were silent and as Beocarn neared where the end should be, he became uneasy and mild panic set in. It was just about break time he thought to himself, nothing to be alarmed about. He tried to calm himself down as best as he could assuring himself that there must be a reason.

After calming himself slightly he was hit suddenly by a strong stench emanating from further down the tunnel. The smell stung his nostrils and reminded him of a hart he found dead and decaying on a path in the Serpentine Mountains during his youth. His pace became more hurried as he searched for the source of the smell. Ahead in the tunnel, he could see what looked like a chamber which was lit up with a strong purple glow. As he approached the doorway the smell became overwhelming causing him to pull his tunic up over his face. When first peered into the room he let out a gasp. Inside the floor was littered with the bodies of dwarven miners. This was different though, these bodies looked as though they had been decomposing for months which wasn't possible.

Near the center of the chamber sat the source of the glowing, a fist-sized deep purple gem that was laying among the bodies. It was glowing with such intensity that the entire chamber was lit up with a purplish hue. As Beocarn stared at the gem he began to feel nauseated. He felt lightheaded at first but that turned into a strobe of several disturbing images in his head. Among the images of decaying faces, dwarves and animals one image stuck out. It was of a giant pyramid made of the same purple gemstone. A voice from inside beckoned for Beocarn to let go of his burden and to join them inside. As Beocarn came to his senses he realized he was walking slowly towards the stone. He felt as though he had no control of his body as it made its way over.

As he reached out his hand towards the stone to grab it a huge wave of dread washed over him, and his heart sank in his chest. He pulled his hand away as if from some sort of flame and scrambled to come up with a plan. Near one of the bodies was a lifting pouch. It was used by the miners to make heavy gems and minerals lighter for transport back. The bags themselves are made with fine dwarven linen imbued with lodestone which gives it it's magical properties. Beocarn hoped the magical enchantment would protect him from the destructive forces of the stone. He picked up the pouch which was a fair size and threw it over the stone, so it was inside. He then gently rolled the stone into the bag and tied the top shut. His plan seemed to work, and the effects of the stone had not done in Beocarn yet. This was some serious magic so Beocarn knew he had to get this gem to someone who would be able to tell him how to neutralize it. More stones like this, if they were discovered, could lay waste to the cities of the dwarves. Beocarn needed to find an elf to help him figure out what this was and fast. The dwarves use magic for enchantments and to make mining easier, but this was beyond even their knowledge.

Beocarn made his way out of the tunnel and straight to his house on the outskirts of the city. He stopped only long enough to grab some supplies for his journey, a short sword he named Sliver, some food and a canteen. Sliver was a short sword made of steel and imbued with a sort of magical poison that drained the energy of anyone struck with it. After grabbing supplies Beocarn made his way out of the city south and towards the elven and human lands. His destination was a city called Twill'Bru in the elvish tongue. The city had a growing human population and it was one of the only places left that humans and elves live together in the entire empire.

Being in a hurry Beocarn simply took a pony from a nearby farm using a saddle he had found in their barn. He left lodestone worth over six thousand gold pieces in the barn with a well-written note. The note explained the urgency and thanked the farmers for helping him to save the dwarves from certain peril.

Once on the pony, Beocarn made his way south along the dwarven roads which lead to a highway used to get to Twill'Bru. By this time dusk was setting in and to the west, Beocarn could see the Tower of the Ancients rising from the landscape. The tower was carved out of white marble and gilded. The setting sun playing off of those features was quite the sight to behold and it was the first time that Beocarn felt himself relax a little bit and his shoulders slumped slightly.

A little over an hour after he passed the tower Beorcarn approached the edge of Twill'Bru. The houses here were clearly inspired by elven design but many had fallen into disrepair. Beocarn made his way along the main road of the city found himself a pub that looked like it might have what he needs, a good stiff drink. After tying up his pony outside, Beocarn made his way in with the lifting pouch slung over his shoulder. The air inside was thick with smoke and the smell of cooking meat. Most of the patrons were humans and had flagons of ale or mead in their hands and were loudly cheering, drinking and dancing. Among the chaos at a table, a young elf sat by himself. His flagon of ale was untouched, and he sat staring at it as if lost in thought. This is exactly what Beocarn needed an elf that he could ask for advice. Beocarn made his way over to the table and spoke shyly in his best elvish, "Hello, my name is Beocarn. I have a question I really need to ask you."

The young elf looked up from his ale and replied to the dwarf, "Hello Beocarn, my name is Drens. What is it that you want to know?" As Drens finished his eyes welled up with tears. Beocarn pulled out a chair sat down and began to his story.

Chapter 5

Ciaran was laying on his bedroll inside his tent when he was jolted up by a loud trill from the signal stone stowed away in his saddlebag. He jumped to his feet and ran to the bag opening it and removing the stone. He uttered the answering phrase aloud to activate it "Atravaar."

The stone glowed brighter as a voice came through on the other side. It was that of Garswick the mayor of Brambleton, or Twill'Bru as the elves call it. "Hello Sir Ciaran," Garswick yelled through the stone. "How are the preparations coming along, my friend?"

"Very good," Carswell replied proudly. "We are poised to make serious gains and I want to thank you again for all your help."

"Don't get too ahead of yourself chief we got a big problem. That damned Bandit King has decided he wants to attack my city. That is gonna end up bad for the both of us. So, I say we change the plan slightly." Garswick stated with concern in his voice.

"That's not good at all," Ciaran replied, "We are going to have to mobilize and stop them. We can't lose Brambleton it is key to this campaign."

"Good, good," Carswell said relieved by the news. "I hope to see you soon then." As the transmission ended the light inside the stone faded and Garswick was gone. Carswell rose to his feet and began to pack for the road. He would leave his second in command, Jerold, in charge of the forces while he went to deal with this issue. He would take with him only a small unit of six thousand soldiers to help fend off the bandit invasion coming from the south.

Within a half an hour of being notified Carswell was off on his fastest horse and with six thousand soldiers in tow including cavalry, mage eaters and battle faeries. One such faerie had been sent ahead to Brambleton to warn the human forces stationed there to form up ahead of time. To move the entire unit, he had brought with him in position in time would take nearly an entire day so Carswell and his thousand-plus cavalry rode ahead and left the bulk of the unit behind to make their way at their pace.

After a few hours of hard riding west, Carswell and the cavalry arrived at the edge of Brambleton where they were greeted by a large division of troops that had been rallied from the city. It was a mixture of elves in traditional armour who numbered around six hundred. About six thousand human soldiers were also rallied, they were wearing traditional human armour but adorned with the colours of Brambleton. Carswell had been secretly funding this small army through bribes paid to Carswell for years and it was finally paying off. Carswell wasted no time in taking control of these forces and beginning to move them to the defensive positions south of the city. On his way through the city, Carswell was waved down by Garswick and he stopped his horse jumping off to the ground. He walked up to the mayor and the two shook hands.

"I know we have much catching up to do but I must introduce you to someone," Garswick said as he motioned Carswell towards Drens who was standing behind the mayor with Beo-

carn beside him holding his bag. "This is the guy who discovered the plot so to speak, kids a hero if you ask me. Thought
you may wanna shake his hand." Garswick grumbled.

Before Carswell had a chance to reach out for a hand-
shake Drens blurted out, "I think we might have something
that could win this easily," and looked at the bag slung over
Beocarn's shoulder. Beocarn shot Drens a look of disapproval
and lowered his head. "Sir, would we be able to talk to you pri-
vately?" Drens enquired.

"Sure thing," Carswell replied nodding to Garswick.

Garswick looked around at everyone's faces and said,
"Ok," before walking away back towards his office.

Once they were alone Drens opened up to Carswell. "This
is my new friend Beocarn. He found something quite powerful
and is trying to find a way to destroy it. I thought maybe before
we do that, we could use this thing to win the battle that is
coming."

"What is this 'thing' you speak of?' asked Carswell curi-
ously.

"A stone," Drens started.

"It's not just a stone," Beocarn interrupted in a low emo-
tionless voice. "It's more than that, it's evil."

"We can use it to defeat the bandits and then we can make
sure we destroy it. I know exactly where we need to go to de-

stroy it for good. There will be a mage strong enough at Mwel'Po." Drens implored.

"The Tower of the Ancients? I passed it on my way here. I say we just leave this place before it gets attacked and make our way there. Even if we want to use it as a weapon, we would be better off finding out how to control it first. Maybe they can help there." Beocarn said as tried to reason with Drens.

Carswell after taking some time to weigh this new development stated, "If this stone is as powerful as you say it is then I also say we go north to the Tower of the Ancients. The mages of the Tower have a strong grasp of magic and can really help us better understand what it is we are dealing with. I will oversee the defences being put into place and then we can ride before sunset towards the Tower."

The three all nodded in agreement and Carswell turned, jumped back on his horse and left south towards the southern wall. Drens and Beocarn returned to the pub to wait for Carswell's return.

***

A few hours later in the pub, Beocarn had become blind drunk, "Will you escort me to go urinate? I don't feel safe." He pleaded with Drens.

"Aye," Drens replied and the two made their way outside and into a suitable alleyway nearby. There was a drain at the base of one of the walls and Beocarn made his way over and began to urinate with Drens watching the way they came in.

As Beocarn finished, a dishevelled looking human walked into the alleyway. "What you got in the bag dwarf?" he demanded as he approached. In his right hand, he had a very large dagger. Drens fell back to beside Beocarn and drew his sword. Beocarn reached for his sword and as he pulled it out the bag slipped off his shoulder and fell to the ground. As it did the top came open and the stone came tumbling out. Its glow filled the alleyway and the thief's eyes became wide with wonder. He approached the stone and reached out for it.

"Don't touch it!" Beocarn warned but it was too late. The thief grasped the stone in his hand but was unable to lift it. Though only the size of a fist it was extremely dense, weighing what Beocarn guessed to be around five hundred units. Within seconds of pulling on the stone, the thief began to glow purple as well, every vein in his body now visible through his skin and clothing. A giant flash of purplish magic consumed his body and then he fell to the ground as a rotting cadaver. The stone had caused him to fully decay in a matter of seconds. Drens now cowered in the corner behind Beocarn who quickly grabbed his bag from the ground and threw it over the stone again. A few seconds later and he had it secured back inside. That was when Beocarn noticed Carswell, standing at the end of the alleyway with his sword drawn. His eyes had glazed over, and his face betrayed his level of disbelief in what he had just seen.

Drens walked forward now and broke the silence between them, "I changed my mind, this thing needs to be destroyed. It is far too powerful and could just as easily be used against us." he reasoned.

"Ok well we should leave now before he gets here," Beocarn added.

The two of them looked at Carswell whose eyes were still glazed over who replied with a monotone, "Yes, it must be destroyed."

Chapter 6

It was not until they had passed the last farmstead outside of Brambleton that the trio slowed from a gallop. The Tower was still a good hour and a half ride north, so they made their way as quickly and quietly as possible. Beocarn now had his lifting pouch attached to his pony's saddle and had it squeezed between his left leg and side of the animal. None of the three people spoke a word the entire way to the Tower.

Upon arriving at the foot of the Tower Beocarn let out another loud gasp as he had before. Even with all the splendour of the dwarven cities, he had never seen anything like this before. The face of the walls was completely smooth which scattered the light that hit it giving the Tower a warm glow.

Drens approached the guards standing outside of the entrance and addressed them in elvish, "We have an emergency and we must speak with the High Mage as soon as possible."

"What emergency?" one of the guards inquired with a stern look across his face. He tightened his grip on the halberd at his side.

Beocarn undid the top of the lifting bag and revealed just a sliver of stone within. The guard's face changed, and a look of concern washed over it. He ushered the three inside and sent a page to let the High Mage know he had visitors. The trio waited for the High Mage in the bottom floor which was littered with various flasks for potions and tomes of various sizes.

A young page made his way down the stairs and announced, "The High Mage is ready to see you now." The trio made their way up the ornate staircase towards the High Mage's chambers on the floor above them. The High Mage's chamber was also littered with scrolls and tomes. A large wooden desk sat to one end of the room and a magically imbued lamp sat atop it illuminating the room. The High Mage sat behind his desk and watched the three men enter his chambers.

"So, what is the emergency that brings you to me? What is this item that you carry with you?" the High Mage asked with his eyes focused on the bag slung over Beocarn's shoulder.

Beocarn stepped forward and placed the bag on the mage's desk and took a step back before explaining. "My name is Beocarn sir, I am from Lalhaal in the Serpentine Mountains. I was working as a runner in the Glimmermine and one day I arrived at work to find everyone had disappeared. When I investigated, I found this stone in a newly uncovered chamber surrounded by the bodies of a dozen or so of my fellow dwarves. I found the stone drawing me to touch it, so I panicked and threw it into a lifting pouch. I then left my home in search of an elf to help me decipher what it was and what had happened to my friends. I found this young elf in Twill'Bru and he directed me to come here and consult you. Our human friend has helped us get here promptly because a rebel Elven army marches on Twill'Bru as we speak. Please can you help us?"

The High Mage inhaled sharply and brought his hand to his face. He then replied Beocarn in a deep gravelly voice and speaking perfect dwarven, "You have done well young one. Your actions may have saved the lives of thousands. Without even laying eyes on this item I can tell you that it a very dangerous item." his gaze now turned to the bag on his desk. He reached out and undid the top of the bag and slowly opened it so that he could look inside at the stone itself. Its glow illuminated his face and he stared for some time into the bag before closing it and retying the top. "Very dangerous indeed," he said slumping into his chair slightly. "I have never seen such a concentration of death and entropy before. You are right to seek the destruction of this item. I believe it is the Ybon Stone from legend. This is no ordinary artifact or magical weapon. It is simply a pure concentrated form of death magic."

"How do we destroy it then?" Beocarn asked shakily.

The High Mage answered him in a very serious tone, "You and your friends must take the stone and bring it to sacred waters adjacent to the Tower. There is a small ritual that must be performed, and the waters will drain away all of the evil concentrated within and neutralize it," the High Mage then pulled a scroll from one of the drawers in his desk and handed it to Beocarn. "This is the ritual that you must perform, please use haste so that we can make sure this evil never takes hold in this world."

Beocarn took the scroll from the Mage and put it aside in his cloak. He then took the lifting pouch from the desk and turned to his friends. As he turned a loud war horn sounded interrupting the moment. Concerned the High Mage waved his arms and a viewing portal appeared before him. It showed the area around the Tower and a large bandit force was forming just outside the Tower's wards. "Don't worry," the High Mage assured them, "there are magical wards that protect this place. They will not be able to break them. Take the stone and the scroll, there is a secret exit that will take you out to the edge of the water below."

Carswell turned to his companions, "You two go and complete the ritual, I will hold off Kalraxix and his men."

"They will kill you," Beocarn pleaded with Carswell. "Come with us."

"The only thing that matters is that the stone gets destroyed. I will make sure to keep the Bandit King distracted until that happens." Carswell assured them. With that, the trio left the High Mage's chambers with Carswell heading to the entrance and the other two descended on a ladder from the first floor to a tunnel below the surface. The tunnel was hewn from the rock and was unlit. The walls were covered in mineral deposits from the water running down the sides. Beocarn and Drens walked the dark tunnel for some time before a faint light could be seen on the other side. As the two stepped out of the tunnel they were hit by a fresh breeze coming off the water. Before them stood the sacred waters, which were teeming with life. In the distance, they could hear the bandits and their horses but for now, they were alone. They set up a small temporary camp near the edge of the water and began to prepare for the ritual. Beocarn began to read the steps of the ritual while Drens watched his back.

Chapter 7

Several hours passed and Beocarn was no closer to figuring out the ritual. Even with the help, Drens parts of the incantation were indecipherable. The pair began to panic as the gravity of the situation weighed on them. The sounds of the bandit army had long since faded and dusk was beginning to set in.

"What if we simply submerge it? Bag and all," Beocarn suggested. "That may do the trick."

"I have a feeling that wouldn't help," Drens replied his face contorted by a mixture of fear and anxiety. "What if it just leaked in the water making everything worse?"

Unable to decide on a course of action the two sat beside the water's edge pouring over the scroll. Unknown to them a small group of five bandits had made their way down to the water and spotted the elf and dwarf. Stealthily they made their way over to them and staged an ambush. The leader of the group gave a signal and they jumped out of the shadows to confront the pair who were huddled over the water.

Drens quickly scrambled to a fighting position and drew

his sword. Beocarn followed suit and also drew his sword which glowed purple when unsheathed, the lifting pouch lay at his feet. All five of the bandits lurched forward to attack at once. Drens was able to deflect the sword of the closest one and plunged his sword deep into his chest with one swift motion causing him to slump to the ground.

Beocarn meanwhile defended himself from two of the bandits and managed to land a strike on the hand of one of the bandits. The wound began to burn with the intensity of a forge's fire and weakness took over the bandit's body. He fell to his knees and Beocarn wasted no time in opening his throat sending him to the ground convulsing violently. Drens facing two bandits himself was able to easily deflect all of the blows.

A sixth bandit who had been hiding nearby in a shrub then loosed an arrow towards Dren. The arrow struck Dren in neck sending him spinning to the side, but he was able to catch himself and face his attackers again. One of the bandits tried to seize on this opportunity and took a big swing at Drens which he easily deflected. Drens drove his sword up through the bandit's throat and out the top of his skull killing him instantly. The archer bandit lost another arrow this time hitting Drens in the back. The arrow made it all the way through and was sticking out of the front of Drens' chest. In a single motion, Drens turned and cut the throat of the last bandit fighting him and then ran full speed at the archer with his sword drawn. Drens let out a booming battle cry which echoed off the cliff face. The archer was able to lose another arrow this time hitting Drens in the center of his chest. Drens lost no momentum and a moment later found himself on top of the archer. The archer struggled to react in time and Drens wasted no time burying his sword into his face. Drens felt himself waver but was able to steady himself for a moment but a dizzy spell sent him to the ground.

Beocarn found himself now fighting alone against the leader of the group. Beocarn was no swordsman so he found himself simply deflecting blows from the elf who was much larger than himself. One of the blows knocked Beocarn's sword from his hands.

As Beocarn reached for his sword the bandit put his foot on it and held his blade up to the dwarf's neck. "Where is the artifact?" the bandit leader asked in a commanding tone. "Give it to me and I may let you live."

Beocarn looked at the elf standing over him, licked the blood from his lips and spat at the elf's feet. "I would never help an animal like you," the dwarf proclaimed proudly, a wry grin appearing on his face.

"Very well," the bandit replied, raising his sword up with both hands above his head, "then you die." The bandit began to bring his sword down towards Beocarn when his eyes opened wide in surprise and he let out a gasp. A blade punched out through the front of his chest and after a moment he slumped to the ground in a pile before Beocarn. Behind his stood Drens with his sword in hand. He was barely able to stand and with his task done he fell to his knees holding himself upright with his sword. When he tried to speak no sounds came out except for an unsettling gurgling noise.

Beocarn ran to his friends' side and wrapped his arms around him, "You saved me, friend, now let's get you somewhere to rest this does not look good."

Carswell suddenly appeared out of the darkness and addressed his companions, "There you are."

Beocarn was relieved to see Carswell and pleaded with him, "We need to get Drens some help, the bandits did a number on him. I would be dead if it were not for him. Please we can't let him die here like this." Carswell's face remained expressionless as he came closer. Beocarn noticed his eyes were still glazed over and a wave of fear washed over him again. "Ciaran, are you ok?" the dwarf asked.

Carswell kneeled over Drens who lay in a pool of his own blood struggling to breathe. He stroked the elf's face gently before producing a dagger from under his cloak. Before Beocarn had time to react Carswell used the dagger to cut Drens throat.

Blood flowed freely from the wound and Drens began to convulse on the ground.

Beocarn stumbled backwards in disbelief, "Why? Why would you do that?" he pleaded with Carswell as he scrambled to get to his feet and draw his sword once more. As Carswell walked towards him Beocarn backed up to gain distance. While doing so he tripped upon a rock and fell on his back. As the human loomed over him, he took a swing which was deflected.

Carswell stepped on the dwarf's arm pinning him in place and then raised his sword up for a strike. "I truly am sorry," he said before driving the sword through Beocarn's chest. The dwarf let out one last sigh and then his body went lifeless. Carswell removed his sword from the dwarf's chest and walked over the edge of the water where the lifting pouch lay. He picked up the bag and slung it over his shoulder before walking off back into the darkness.

***

Not far from the foot of the Tower of the Ancients outside of the wards the Bandit King had made camp. A large bonfire burned in the center of the camp and was surrounded by the King and his officers. Some of the officers were celebrating their recent victories in the south and were enjoying a few drinks. Not Kalraxix, he was deep in thought and seemed troubled. As the merriment continued, they were suddenly alerted to the presence of a human man walking up towards their bonfire. It was Lord Carswell who was carrying with him a bag. As he approached Kalraxix broke his silence, "Were you successful?" he inquired.

"Yes," replied Carswell taking the bag off his shoulder and placing it at the King's feet. "It's in the bag. It is a lot heavier than it looks," he warned.

Kalraxix's face changed and a smile took over it. He turned and dismissed his officers with a motion of his hand, and they wasted no time leaving the two leaders alone at the fire. Once alone Kalraxix addressed Carswell, "We have our deal than human," he stated, "In return for your support and this generous gift I will recognize your rule over all of the eastern lands." he lay a hand on Carswell's shoulder before continuing, "You must be very proud human, the hegemony of the elves over your people has finally come to an end."

Without saying a word Lord Carswell turned and left in the same direction he had come from. He got back onto his horse and set off in the direction of Brambleton to meet up with his army.

Chapter 8

Kalraxix sat alone in a room lit with a few dozen candles.

On the table in front of him sat the lifting pouch containing the Ybon Stone. During his research since acquiring the stone, Kalraxix had discovered an ancient spell that could be used to summon Ybon, the god of death and darkness. Feeling he had read enough about how the ritual was done the Bandit King prepared. He lay the scroll containing the ritual out on the table. He then untied the top of the lifting pouch and dumped the Ybon Stone out on the table before him. He was not worried as his elvish blood protected him from the most disastrous effects of the stone.

Placing his right hand on the stone caused its magic to course through him. Once a magical bridge was formed, he uttered the incantation, "Ybon ress trawlik." As he did so a bright purple light grew inside his hand and travelled up his arm. The energy pooled in his head and caused his eyes to glow bright purple. Kalraxix let out one last scream before collapsing face down on his table.

When he lifted his head again, he had been taken over completely by the dark lord Ybon. The dark lord was pleased by this turn of events and exclaimed, "Finally after thousands of years I am free of that prison. It is time now to complete my plans." the bright purple faded from his eyes and he called for his officers to join him in his study.

Three of his best men arrived in the study for what they

thought was news about the ongoing civil war. Ybon spoke to them through the body of Kalraxix, "My brothers your loyalty and strength have helped us in our war effort. We have been able to carve large chunks of territory from the oppressive regime that rules from Fell. Today is a turning point in that fight. No longer will we cower, beg and scrape by. We have a new weapon that will make us unstoppable in the battles to come." As he finished speaking, he gestured towards his officers and purple-hued lightning left his fingertips striking the officers. They screamed out in pain and all three fell to the ground writhing in pain.

They lay on the floor for a minute or more before slowly lifting themselves up and standing before the King once more. The magic Ybon used had transformed them. Their skin had changed to a very dark purple. Their once golden hair had become bone white. Their mouths were full of razor-sharp pointed teeth. Their eyes, once a beautiful blue colour were now blood red. All of this put a rather large smile on the face of Ybon.

"My children," Ybon said affectionately. "It is time that we took that which rightfully belongs to us. The blood of dragons now courses through your body. The world will cower in fear before the mighty Drow!"

Together all of them began to laugh maniacally. Once they

had settled Ybon sent his officers out to gather the rest of his units so that they too could be transformed.

***

Far away, safely inside the Tower of the Ancients, sat the High Mage watching the scene unfold before him through a viewing portal. A very concerned look crossed his face and his heart sank. The elvish empire had stood for over a thousand years but was now at great risk of crumbling. A civil war that had raged for years severely weakened them and they would be unable to face this new threat. They stood to lose most if not all of their territory in the coming years.

The High Mage turned to a very concerned looking page who was standing near the door to his chambers, "It is time that we prepared young one, there is much that needs to be done." he said lowering his tone to match the seriousness of the situation, "May Yuleywa grant us strength and wisdom in these troubling times. This no doubt marks the end of the Elven Era."

The young page ran off to make preparations and the High Mage sat for a moment in silence before getting up to leave himself. As he left through the doorway, he waved his arm and the lamp on his desk dimmed until it went out completely leaving the room in darkness.

ES'FELL
EASTERN ELVEN LANDS
MWEL'PO
(TOWER OF THE ANCIENTS)
FORT CARSHAAS
LAKE ELEYWA
MANNSEND
FORT NORDHAAS
TWILL'BRU
(BRAMBLETON)
WO'VA
(WEST PORT)
CARSTON
FORT HAWURHAAS
IK GRANDIA
BADPORT

THE WOODS
ABIGAIL RABISHAW

This piece was originally a runner up in Carleton University's 2019 Fiction Competition.

Liz found it first. The body.

We were looking for frogs in last year's leaves lining the creek in the forest near our house. Liz's tiny hand emerged from the mulch clutching something wet and shiny. I thought it was a slug.

"Becca? What's this?" She dropped it in my palm.

I stared at what was unmistakably a severed finger. Pale, bloated flesh was barely clinging to the bone. I screamed, and flung it towards the creek.

"Come on, Liz. We're going home. Now." I grabbed Liz's arm and began dragging her away from the creek.

"Becca, stop," she whined. "I don't wanna go home yet."

I ignored her. I scooped her up, despite her protests, and ran out of the woods. I only slowed down when we back on our street, the trees far behind us. I put Liz back down.

"Becca?"

"Yeah?"

"Should we tell mom?"

"You can't tell anyone about that Liz. Do you wanna get in trouble? I sure don't, not for something like that. That's serious stuff. The police will figure it."

Liz nodded solemnly.

I sighed. I didn't know if I was making a mistake, but I sure as shit didn't want to end up in juvie, or something. What if I got in trouble for throwing the finger back?

By the time we got home, Liz was asking about ice cream. She had already mostly forgotten about the finger. Her six-year-old brain was preoccupied with more important things, like deciding between strawberry or chocolate.

By the end of the summer, I had mostly forgotten about it too. Sure, I told Greg, the kid who lived next door, when he asked why I didn't want to go look for frogs with him. But other than that, the finger barely crossed my mind.

Until October. When they found the rest of the body.

I woke up to mom softly knocking on my bedroom door. She opened the door before I could answer, like always, but something felt off.

"Mom?" I asked, groggy. Normally she was gone for work by now, but she was only half ready, with her hair done but still in pajamas. I noticed tears streaked down her cheeks.

"Honey, we're going to stay home today. Something happened at the creek."

My stomach sank. I already knew what she was going to say.

"They found... someone. In the creek. The whole neighbourhood is taped off while they, uh, search for the... rest. Of the person. The girl. So we're going to stay home today, okay honey?"

I stared at her for a minute, before lurching forward, suddenly sobbing. I buried my face in her stomach.

"It's my fault, Mom. This summer, Liz and I... we found... found... a finger," I sobbed.

"What?" Mom tried lifting me out of her lap.

"Baby, what are you saying? You found something this summer?"

"Am I gonna go to jail?"

"No, oh my god. Of course not. But if you found something, we need to go to the police, right now. Okay?"

I shot straight up, eyes wide. Terrified.

"You're sure they're not gonna send me to jail?"

My mom took my hand and smiled a small smile. "Of course not. Can you be brave for me and come tell the police about what you and Liz found?"

I swallowed the lump in my throat and nodded. I had to fix this. I had to help.

Mom helped me put on my coat over my pyjamas, something she hadn't done since I was small. It was fitting though, since I felt smaller than I ever had before.

We left the house and started walking down the street, towards the forest. There were more police cars and officers than I had ever seen. There were even dogs. I thought that only happened in the movies.

We approached an officer standing near the yellow tape crossing the edge of the forest.

"Excuse me?" Mom called out to her. "My daughter just told me something I think might be important."

The officer walked over to us. She bent down to be closer to my eye level.

"Yes, sweetie?" She had kind eyes.

"Um. This summer, when me and Liz- that's my little sister- when we were, uh, looking for frogs in the creek... we found a, um. A finger. Just a finger. With no body."

The cop's kind smile turned serious. She turned away from me and spoke into the radio clipped to her chest. After a few minutes, she came back to me.

"What's your name?" she asked.

"Becca... Rebecca."

"Well, Becca. My name is Carrie. Do you think you could help me out? I want you to show me exactly where you and Liz were this summer. It would be a huge help. Do you think you could do that for me?"

I looked up at my mom, then back at Carrie. I nodded.

Carrie lifted the police tape for me, and reached out for my hand. I took it, and went back into the forest with her for the first time since we found the finger.

Another officer with a giant German Shepherd joined us.

"Do you like dogs?" Carrie asked me. I nodded.

"This is Fremi," She pointed at the dog. "It means protector."

That made me feel better. I smiled at Fremi. He would protect me.

After a few minutes, we got to the area where Liz and I were looking for frogs. I shuddered.

"It was here, in the leaves. I got scared when Liz gave it to me, so I threw it in the creek. I'm sorry."

Carrie squeezed my hand.

"You've been so brave Becca. Thank you so much. Let's get you out of here and back home now, okay?"

We headed back to where my mom was standing, talking to a different officer. As we left the woods, I glanced back over my shoulder. That was the last time I'd ever set foot in them. And that was perfectly fine with me.

Weeks later, the cops were still there. The first thing they found was a foot. Then, the finger Liz and I had tossed back in the creek months earlier. Then another foot, that didn't match the first one. That's when things got real serious. The street was swarmed with cops, every day. All in all, they pulled over a dozen bodies from the creek and the woods surrounding it. It was a wonder we only found the finger, and not something worse.

Around the same time the cops came, we stopped seeing Greg around. His dad didn't want him out and about, apparently. His dad had been to jail a few years before, so we didn't think much of it at the time. Until the cops showed up at Greg's door.

Liz and I were building a snow fort in the yard when they came. I recognized Carrie, and waved at her.

"Why don't you girls head inside? I don't think you should be out here right now," she called over to us. I grabbed Liz and we headed in.

A few minutes later, we heard screaming. I ran over to the window facing Greg's house, and saw them leading his dad out of the house, his hands cuffed behind his back.

I found out years later that they found Greg's mom in the creek. She had gone missing years earlier, but the case went cold. Greg's dad confessed to her murder, as well as all the other girls they found in the woods. Greg left town to live with his aunt, and the woods were never the same again.

WANTED
ANALISA SALITURO

He doesn't see me. He never will. Not like I see him. I wonder what he would do if he could read my mind, if he could see everything I never said. Where we would go from there; what would transpire. Would we fall madly in love and settle down together? Would we try things out, but ultimately fail to make things work? Would he fill the vacancy in my heart? If only he knew I was waiting for him to fill it. If only he knew.

The only comfort I seek is in his face, in his heart. He is kind, he is gentle, he is caring, he is beautiful; everything I don't deserve. In all honesty, I can't say I've done anything to deserve him noticing me. It still shocks me when I see him, and my heart yearns for his. The crazy sensation tingles my whole body, turning my stomach to butterflies and letting go of all other reason. I pretend we would make a perfect couple when in reality he deserves much better. I'm rude, sarcastic, lousy company and, to be blunt, plain. I'm not ugly per se but I'm definitely not beautiful, not even close.

I imagine scenarios in my head where he notices me, notices who I am and loves me anyway. I imagine him recognizing that I am made up of faults but finding the good in me. I imagine him calling me everyday just to tell me how special I am, always ending with his various ways of "I love you."

I abruptly remind myself there is no way that could happen. No way he would ever even take the time to ask my name, let alone search for my deepest secrets. He will not be the one I open up to; he will not save me. He will merely serve as the boy that never was, the boy that could have been. The boy I thought I loved but hardly knew.

TRAILBLAZER
SHELBY VAN PELT

My calves burn and my chest heaves. I'm not so young anymore and this isn't as easy as it used to be. My head pounds, but we keep going. I want to get to the top. I'm sure you do too.

It's a beautiful day for hiking. Summer has sucked the trail dry of spring's mud and a breeze whispers through the tree-tops, washing us in evergreen perfume.

We hike in silence, but for the scuff of boots over roots. Nearby an unseen river, swollen with snowmelt, charges through the forest. As the trail climbs the river's roar fades in and out as if someone is fiddling with its volume knob.

I remember one time you led us up this trail, all of us, when we were kids. Lainey tripped and gashed her knee, and all three of us shouted at you: *Dad, stop, stop, stop!* But your bad ears; you couldn't hear. When Scotty and I finally caught up to you we were panting so hard we could barely talk.

You picked the gravel from Lainey's gash, then tied your handkerchief around her knee and lifted her onto your shoulders. The two of you looked like some bizarre double-decker monster tromping through the woods. Lainey squealed with delight, ducking under the low branches.

This trail is yours. You created it.

After the war you joined the park service. Somewhere in a drawer at home I have an old photo of you standing on a hillside with some other men whose names I don't remember, axes resting on your lean shoulders. You'd be gone for weeks during the summer, that much I do remember. Blasting tunnels for roads, blazing trails, building bridges and picnic shelters. You never missed a mountain summer.

Folded in my back pocket is the glossy brochure the ranger handed me this morning along with the receipt for our twenty-dollar entrance fee. Over two million visitors a year, it says. But we haven't come across another soul on this trail. It's not one of the popular ones.

The terrain starts to steepen, the trees thin. We come around a curve and startle a marmot. It glares at us before trundling off into the undergrowth.

It was the war that took your ears. You were portside when starboard caught a torpedo. The ship sank. You always said you were the luckiest bastard on that boat, hauled off needing only hearing aids.

Your ears got worse over the years. As we kids got older we learned to holler louder, but we also became fluent in your gestures. We knew to nod when we were ready for the pitch and we knew that your stacked fists meant choke up on the bat. We knew to go bother our mother when your lips hemmed together, and we knew that a squeeze on the shoulder at bedtime meant: *I love you.*

The three of us, we were lucky too.

Well, here we are. The trail's end.

I shade my eyes with my hand as I take in the valley. Rows of soft green foothills brushed with purple heather. It's lovely, but as far as vistas on this mountain go, it's humdrum. Other trails are flashier. We could've reached a towering waterfall, a mirrored lake, a mammoth glacier nestled in the shadow of the sleeping volcano itself.

But this trail was always your favorite.

I set my pack down, gently, and sit on the big rock. Of course, there'd be room for all of us on the big rock. But they couldn't make it.

They tried. Lainey got stuck with some so-called work thing, last-minute. And Scotty? Well, you know Scotty. All three of us share blame for putting this off, but I promise, they did want to be here. I'm sorry they're not. I'm sorry it's just me.

You've been in this shoebox three years, Dad. I couldn't let you miss another mountain summer.

At the edge of the hillside I wait for a breeze. Chickadees chatter in the treetops, or maybe they're kinglets or thrushes? I never could tell the difference. You would have known.

I tip the box. The ashes come out in a clump, which tumbles downhill. Panic seizes me. The clump stops under the broad, feathered frond of a huge fern. No, no, no. This is nothing like I'd imagined, nothing like the cinematic scattering of dust on the wind.

It's crazy, but I consider scrambling down to retrieve you. To try again. After all, you hammered that into us, didn't you? If at first you don't succeed? But when I inch my boot down the hillside I set off a small avalanche of dirt and rocks. It skitters down the hill, burying the fern.

You never said what you wanted. By the time Lainey and Scotty and I assembled at your bedside you were nearly gone. Afterward, we brainstormed the plan to bring you here, to set you adrift over the meadow. We thought you would've liked that.

But now I've done the opposite. I've buried you.

I notice the birds have quieted. A distant groan of thunder. Soon the parched dirt will melt to mud. You'll dissolve in the muck. You'll percolate deep, deep, deeper, into the heart of the hillside, maybe into the core of the sleeping volcano itself.

I smile. I think you would have liked that, too.

How I wish I could stay to watch, but it's turned into a terrible day for hiking. The weather can change fast up here in the mountains. Another thing you hammered into us.

To the dark beat of thunderclaps, I hurry back down your trail.

INSPIRATION IN A MINOR
NATHANIEL NEIL WHELAN

The unending hubbub burrows into Jaspar's brain, derailing his train of thought. It's been this way ever since they moved to the city. There is quiet in the country, not like this tempest of constant clamour. If it's not the paper boy yelling from the street corner, it's the trill of bicycle bells. If not that, then the babble of shoe shiners boring their customers from below his window.

Jasper stares with relentless intensity at the squiggles and blots on the sheet music in front of him. Like a beaver, he gnaws on a pencil. Anyone can draw notes on paper; the trick is turning them into a beautiful melody. What he wants plays in his mind like a distant dream. He taps his foot trying to keep time with the *tock tick* of the metronome, but the uneven *clip-clop* of hooves from outside shatters his sense of rhythm. The pencil slips from between his lips as his cheeks balloon with an unreleased howl of frustration.

"My love?"

Jasper bolts upright and almost tumbles off the piano bench. Through eyes puffy from lack of sleep, he watches his wife amble into the room, a tiny wrapped parcel in her hands.

"I'm getting closer," he says instinctively.

"Are you really this time?"

He side-glances at the messy interpretation of music before him.

Juliette sighs. When she speaks, her voice is soft but firm. "This has to stop."

"I'm almost done. I promise."

"You make the same promise every day. When are your lies going to become truth?"

Jasper pauses. "Our wedding vows said nothing about lying." He offers a weak chuckle, but the slight twitch in his smile turns sour when he notices his wife's frown. "Just a few more days."

Juliette stands poised like a statue beside the empty china cabinet, the afternoon sun showering her with golden light. On her other side, their wedding portrait hangs above a side table with a vase of wilted flowers. She prods a crumpled petal of browning pink. "You've been at this song for months now."

"Composition."

"What?"

"A song is something you sing. A musical composition is for instruments."

Juliette huffs with irritation.

"Composing a masterpiece doesn't happen overnight," Jasper explains.

"I understand. But I'm sure even Beethoven slept."

"You don't know that. Geniuses don't need sleep."

Eyes wide, Juliette feigns awe. "My apologies. I didn't realize I was married to a genius."

Jasper shrugs, choosing to ignore the taunt. He runs his hands through his hair, an attempt to distance his likeness from that of a manic hyena—although he feels certain that no beast of the savanna ever sat at a piano in their cotton long johns.

"All I'm saying is that you've become obsessed. It's not healthy to be… *oh, will you shut that thing off!*"

"What thing?"

Juliette makes a pass for the metronome.

"No! I need it. It helps me keep time."

"Do you know what else keeps time? A clock. Like that one over there. I'm starting to wonder if you can read it. You're awake when you should be asleep. You're asleep when you should be awake. Look at yourself! You're a mess. When was the last time you bathed?"

"I come to bed," Jasper retorts, ignoring her question.

"You didn't last night. Nor the night before that. I get up before dawn and can hear you plinking away in here."

"Must be nicer than waking up to that alarm clock you—"

"Jasper…"

A moment of silent reflection. "It's the only time I can get some quiet. The city is too loud during the day." He makes a vague gesture toward the open window to prove his point. "Besides, I use the soft pedal."

Juliette picks at the brown wrapping covering the small parcel. "That's not the point. You play with your piano more than you do with me."

Jasper winces. He doesn't like such crude language. It's not proper decorum, even between a husband and wife.

"Some nights it feels like you're being unfaithful. Music has become your mistress."

"That's unreasonable."

"Is it? You care more for your music than you do for me. Admit it."

Jasper sighs and tries to refocus his attention. He doesn't have time for such petty squabbles.

"You're a child, Jasper Reed. You can't ignore me and expect our problems to vanish."

He can hear the venom dripping from each word. "If I'm such a child, then leave me."

"Don't talk like that! I'm trying to help."

"I don't need help."

"I'm trying to help us!" Juliette's cheeks burn bright red. "We've sold the last of my grandmother's jewelry. All the china. Our savings are dwindling and—"

"And yet you still have money to buy something for yourself." Jasper indicates the parcel. "What is it? A nice brooch for all the fancy parties we don't attend? A new pair of sapphire earrings?"

"—and I won't be able to teach at the schoolhouse much longer. You need a job."

"I have a job."

"Sitting behind a piano, crumpling up expensive sheet music doesn't pay."

"I tried making my own, but I couldn't get the lines straight enough. Strained my eyes."

Juliette takes a long, steadying breath. He knows he shouldn't provoke her. Despite what she might think, he does feel bad for playing games with her emotions. But isn't she just as guilty for taking out her own frustrations on him?

A single moment of clarity recontextualizes everything: is it fair to accuse her of taking out her frustrations on him when

 The Writers Circle 2

he's the reason for it?

"I think it's time for you to ask Mr. Garland for a job. There might be an opening at the factory."

Barely above a whisper, his voice has lost all life. "I refuse to build pianos so that others can play them."

Their back-and-forth comes to a temporary standstill, the silence broken by the incessant *tock tick* of the metronome and the jumble of noise from outside.

"Remember when you first heard me play?"

Juliette smiles for the first time since entering the room; it's but a tiny curl in the left corner of her mouth, but Jasper considers it a good sign. Unsure whether she'll accept, he offers her a seat on the bench beside him. He exhales with relief when she does.

"At Mr. Donovan's Christmas party," Juliette recalls. "He hired you to perform."

Like something out of Dickens, the ghosts of his past materialize before his eyes: a beer hall packed with joyous merrymakers, a canopy of garland and tinsel strung among the rafters, barrels of ale stacked in the far corner, and a lone musician, playing on a raised platform, guiding the crowd through all the Christmas classics.

"Mr. Donovan must've seen something in me no one else did," he says. "That was my first paying job."

Juliette takes his hand; it's cold as if still affected by the frigid temperature of that night six years ago.

Jasper meets her gaze. "I almost stopped playing the moment you walked in. You looked beautiful in that red dress."

"I made it especially for that night." She picks at a loose thread in the stained frock she now wears. "How times have changed."

He releases her hand. "What do you mean by that?"

A second's hesitation proves to be a second too long.

"Do you regret marrying me?"

There's no more anger in her voice. Instead, Jasper detects a hint of sorrow. "No. I regret what you've become."

An exaggerated harrumph spills past his lips. "I suppose you should've wed Clint after all. Imagine that. You married to a big shot lawyer."

"I didn't love him. My parents did, but I didn't. I fell in love with you. And your talent. Back when you played for fun. Do you even enjoy it anymore?"

Unsure how to answer, Jasper says, "You can't force inspiration."

A gaggle of children pass below their window. Their shouts of a summer being thoroughly enjoyed remind him of the long days spent with his mother at the piano while his friends played outside. But he never minded. Music was all he ever needed.

"I'm scared." He doesn't recognize his own voice—the frailty of it, the vulnerability.

"Of what?"

Tenderly, Jasper places his right hand on his wife's belly. "That my life as a musician is at an end. A few more weeks, Juliette. That's all the time I have left."

And that is the truth laid bare. He sighs, long and hard, as if depleting his lungs entirely of air. It feels good to finally let it out. He's confident he made the right choice in confiding in her, that is until he reads Juliette's expression. A curtain of disappointment descends between them. She rises curtly from the bench.

"I thought this is what you wanted." She indicates the small parcel in her hand and places it indelicately upon the piano next to his sheet music. "Let me know if I was wrong." She departs, heels clacking against the floorboards.

Jasper is left alone. The room is swathed in silence save for the ever-ticking metronome. Even the shouts from outside have momentarily been put to bed. Isn't this what he truly wanted? Some quiet so he could work?

His fingers rest splayed over the black and white keys, but the parcel draws his attention, begging to be opened. Cursing under his breath, Jasper picks it up. It's heavier than it looks.

The tape gives way without resistance. Behind the wrapping is a child's music box embroidered with golden ornamentation. Professionally etched on the lid is a single letter: A.

For Abigail. Or for Adam.

Jasper spares a moment to trace the etching with his thumb before replacing it on top of the piano. His fingers return to the keys, but still, he considers the small box. With a sigh of defeat, he opens the lid.

A porcelain violinist twirls on the end of a tiny spring to dulcet, tinkling music. It seeps into his brain like honeyed sentimentality. Shoulders slack and eyes closed, he envisions the barred paper in front of him, devoid of all cross-outs and scratches—a perfectly balanced combination of notes and rests.

Mindlessly, his fingers travel to the highest octave where they begin to play a variation of the box's melody; it isn't a total recreation, but an accompaniment. It's soft at first, delicate—so fragile in fact that one missed note or unintentional slip threatens to shatter its mesmeric hold on him. The two rhythms complement each other, weaving a warm blanket of such saccharine sound that tears pearl his lower lids.

To Jasper, it seems as if he's been collaborating for years with the miniature violinist to create this very piece of music. It's a composition that's been living inside of him for a while, but has, until now, been playing hide-and-seek.

You can't force inspiration.

Jasper still believes that to be true. Inspiration, that ever-elusive fiend, finds you.

THE TRAIN TO LONDON
LAURA WILSON

I press my back against the wall and look up at the train departures board for the millionth time. Four more minutes.

A couple of teenage boys snicker as they walk by. I wonder what they see when they look at me, train ticket clutched in my damp hands, eyes scanning the platform in barely suppressed panic. I make a conscious effort to straighten up, try to stop shaking.

I'm just a regular person, waiting for my train to London on a Friday after work. Two more minutes. The knot in my stomach tightens. Scott won't be expecting me home for another half an hour. There is no reason for him to suspect I'm at the train station.

As the rumble of the train can be heard in the distance, the others on the platform start moving towards the edge. I stay against the wall and survey my fellow passengers.

Three women in their fifties lugging large suitcases, giggling like schoolgirls. A man in his mid-twenties, around my age, casually dressed with a backpack slung over one shoulder. And a scattering of professionals in business suits, loosening their ties and starting to relax for the weekend ahead.

No Scott.

I take a deep breath and pick up the small overnight bag I had packed that morning. I wince as the bag knocks against my ribs that haven't quite healed from the last time Scott lost his temper.

The rush of wind from the train blows back my hair. Long and blonde. The way Scott likes it. Once I get to Lydia's flat, I am going to make a hair appointment. Ask the hairdresser to chop it all off. Dye it brown. Or maybe black. The thought helps push me forward, away from the safety of the wall.

I keep expecting to feel Scott's hand grabbing at my arm so I run the last few steps to the train and sink into a window seat. I close my eyes until I feel the train start to move and then I pull my mobile phone out of my bag and send a quick text to Lydia: On the train. Thank you so much for letting me stay with you for a while xxx.

"Do you mind if I sit here?" The man I had noticed on the platform gestures to the seat opposite me.

"Sure." My voice sounds shaky and distrustful, but he

grins at me and sits down, putting his backpack on the empty seat beside him.

"Is that the new iPhone?" he asks when he's settled.

"Yeah." Scott had bought it for me last month, presenting it with a flourish, waiting for my pathetic gratitude.

"Cool," the man says and looks at me expectantly, wanting conversation.

But the words freeze in my throat. I picture the last time I had a conversation with a well-meaning man on a train. He had been friendly and very funny. I had paid for my laugh with a bruise on my arm that hurt for days.

"Sorry," the man says, still smiling, not put off by my clumsy silence. "I'm on my way to a mate's wedding. It's the first time I've been away since my son was born, so I'm a bit over-excited."

Scott isn't here, I remind myself.

"How old is your son?" I ask finally.

And just like that, I'm having a conversation. I'm just a regular person on my way to London.

I start to smile. I laugh tentatively when he complains no one warned him of the perils of projectile poo before he decided to have a baby. And when the conductor comes to check our tickets, I hold mine out with a steady hand.

"So what about you?" he asks. "Where are you headed?"

      The Writers Circle 2

I glance out the window at the little rows of houses speeding past.

"Basically," I say, "I'm leaving behind everything that's wrong with my life."

He pauses, waiting to see if I elaborate and when I don't, he starts telling me about the last time he was in London. How his wife wanted one last romantic getaway before the baby was born, but when they got there, she couldn't walk more than five steps without needing to sit down for a rest.

"Where are you headed now?" he asks as the train approaches Liverpool Street Station.

"I'm taking the tube to my friend's house," I say and then I add recklessly, "she lives near Epping."

"No way! I'm going to Epping," he says. And then "My mate's picking me up. Do you want a lift?"

I hesitate. I've only just met this man. I don't even know his name. But he's been so friendly. And he has a wife and a little baby at home.

And today is the start of my new life.

"Yeah, that would be great," I say, pulling my bag onto my lap.

I follow him off the train and through the station. It's crowded and he grabs my arm. I flinch and then force myself to relax. He's only trying to make sure we don't get separated.

I blink in the bright sunlight and he leads me to a car waiting outside the station. He opens the back door for me and I slide inside. I glance at my phone, surprised Scott hasn't called me yet.

The car starts to move and I look back to see my new friend still standing on the pavement. He is smiling.

"Hey, wait," I say, but the driver only speeds up.

I catch his eye in the rearview mirror and blink once, twice. This can't be happening. I reach for the door handle, but I hear the click of the lock.

"Where were you planning to go?" Scott asks.

His voice is calm. Reasonable.

I slump back against the seat and close my eyes.

POETRY

SEMPITERNAL
CASSIDY BEST

Rooibos

I would rather smell like herbal tea and cigarettes
Than fresh perfume and old regrets
Let me choke on smoke and whiskey
To chase the tears stuck in my throat
From reliving the moment
You finally said good-bye

Iced Coffee

Cold coffee, long forgotten

Sitting in purgatory
Quietly yearning for the warmth
That only a hand can provide
Break the spell of ambivalence,
of waiting and watching
the kitchen's goings on like an outsider
With only the simple wish to be held
or at the very least, consumed

Lessons

What they say about creative types is true,
Pay us no mind, do not fall in love
For we immortalize you on paper, in song.
When we two found a kindredness between our hearts –
the art was pure and beautiful
until it turned sour –
The majors become minors; the ink runs red
Is the tragedy really the loss of love,
Or the change in tune?

Addicted

Smoke curls around my tongue the way yours once did
I watch its tendrils twirl from between my lips through the
waiting window
Slipping through my fingers as easily as ours came apart
It's a funny thing, smoking.
I started inhaling poison just to forget you.
Impossible when each drag tastes like a memory
Exhale and all I can think of is the next pull and the next
As if the closer the cherry comes to my face, the closer you'll
be
Instead, I find myself with smoke in my eyes and burns on my
hands
Missing you even more than I did before

BECOMING MEMORY
ROXANNE CARDONA

THE WAIT

It's midnight in late November. Our feet put distance
    between us and the hospital. Our shoes, the only
sound for blocks. We look for an open diner, in order

not to talk about him. Our father. Or the doctor
    who asked, *Do you want me to revive him?*
Like he had hit us with a baseball bat, inside his

green curtained stadium, my father's still strong
    hands gripping the silver bed bars, awake and
not awake. Overhead, the fluorescent light reflects

on my brother's glasses. Dad's life now a coin toss;
    Heads, he lives, *tails — There's a sandwich shop
on Gun Hill,* my brother says. We pass men in front

of bodegas who hold paper cups, smoke cigarettes.
    Smell of burnt coffee, cooked meats. Our legs
warm under the laminate countertop. The sandwiches

grilled brown, cheese spilling from their centers.
     What time do we have to be back? Two a.m.,
I answer. *Remember when Daddy made us eat*

the Limburger cheese? I continue. *How it stunk up*
     the kitchen? A chuckle falling from my brother's
mouth. *Remember how mad Mom got? I remember*

the smell, he says, wipes his nose first with a napkin
     then his mouth, just like our father did. I want to ask,
will he die? *Not too bad, the sandwich,* he says.

He opens the door for me, his yawn slips into
     the blue morning. A half moon guides me forward,
the street light changes from red to green, as we cross.

Crouched together before the dark screen,
my mother and I gaze at the black circles,
floating around like round bugs.
The doctor moves his mouse, it clicks
eating up small pieces of his desk top.
It hovers over a larger beetle-like sphere,
then his voice, *here and here.*

This is my mother's liver, lesion after lesion
polka-dot the charcoal image. He studies us,
our faces, the way my mother purses her lips
as if smiling, the way I purse my lips as if smiling.
I am my mother's daughter. And then the lingo—
it could be,
it could be—
metastatic, secondary
grade, stage, grade, stage.

His answer is to prescribe more.
Tests. Tests. Blood. Blood.
Already, my mother's arms blue and pit.
But he doesn't know my mother.
Or her voice. How she pours out her song
thick and velvety. Slips the busboy
a twenty, for college, she says. Still
carries her groceries over many city blocks.

Alone in the room, I help her out
of the green gown, thread each arm,
through each sleeve. Note how full they are,
how her skin dimples at the elbows.
Smooth the fabric over her stomach. I study
her black hair, curled and thick, the aquiline nose,
her lips still painted in bright pink.
I close my eyes, hear her familiar humming
as we get ready to leave through the hospital doors.

BARK BEETLE

We are more alike than not.
I and the bark beetle
that came crashing into my room
last Saturday evening.

Dramatic, clicking his wings
like metal scissors slicing up
the light from my desk lamp.
Like him, I've never come into a room

unnoticed. Handsome—skinned in knotty
pine, more wall art or wood carving
than insect, most would roll up
a magazine and swat him.

No matter how much
he flaps, or menaces.
I know the he means no harm.
Even when he opens his wings,

a sharp embrace, I know I cannot.
Suddenly, he leaps—
into the blaze of lamp light,
spinning and sputtering,

buzzing —falling backwards
hitting the table with a sound
not unlike a small pot dropping,
becomes a thing missed.

Could I choose fire, pilot this body
filled with blood into the twinning blaze?
I do not feign surprise at his ending.
Just how quickly his life becomes memory.

MY CLASSROOM IS EMPTY

I am the ivory-billed woodpecker sitting at the desk

who plucks her tail away

Critically endangered, my voice crawls up the wall

Hey moonlight, break my heart

Sing the morning anthem, the ones the kids sang

Oh, say can you see—

What is left?   Apparitions cannot

hold air

I'm timed out—

I am that doppelganger

Doctor, if it's not too late

will you prescribe the drink

that will unload my camera?

I think

I've swallowed all the markers

Forgive me, some were red

The purple ones

hurt the most

THREE POEMS
JENNIFER CARR

The Volcano

Sometimes I am tired
of feeling the inferno
bubbling up inside
loud noises
deafening my ears
from the explosions
of lava crashing
silent venomous words awakening
violently shaking my core
red hot molten lava
running, running
down the mountainside
there is no escaping
the heat from the fire
so orange and so red
the silent screams
the insanity in my mind
turning into tears
pouring from my eyes
burning my face

ready to explode
from the inside
to the outside

Evil Forces

calling my name
powerless
defenseless
powerless
vulnerable
am i
unable
to think
feel
express
or love
myself
any longer
why me
i surrender
myself
to you
to evil
forces
not by
choice
warm heart
now cold
a flame
now frozen
the teard
       r
       o
       p
       s

raind
    r
    o
    p
    s
mere d
    r
    o
    p
    s
of existence
who i used
to be
dear god
he has lead me
to dark places
spiritually
i am dead
in darkness
closed doors
open for me
a place to go
but return
my body
comes alive
but the flame
never to be
rekindled

The Silent Intruder

Sneaking around
Time and time again
Looking for an open window
Unlocked front door perhaps
Any loose crevice or corner
The silent intruder will find it
And strike once again
With never any remorse
Anytime of the day or night
The unwelcome guest
Invades my personal space
When I least expect it
Meddling in my mind
Bringing unwanted thoughts
This thief steals my happiness
As these lapses of sanity
Become greater and greater
Panic sets in and I want to fight
But there is just one problem
I have never been a fighter
As I wipe the tears away
My heart is pumping
The terror of being trapped
Alone with this anxiety
is too much to think about
Tangled in this tunnel vision
I must find a way back to sanity

OUR SHORT SEASON
LISA FLECK DONDIEGO

THE FIRST TIME YOU SAW MY HOUSE

you felt sorry for it—like no one lived there—
so you quickened a garden, uprooted

the overgrown vines, tilled beds from the rocks,
put in the first rhododendron, Japanese maples,
spruce, tulips, weeping cherry, climbing roses.

You brought a hummingbird feeder,
a fountain, a bell that tinkled in the wind,
fastened house numbers to our arbor.

Now I try to remember you the way
a garden remembers its roots in winter,
the dogwoods, their flowers,

the morning glories, their days of winding,
but all I can see is the moldering ground,
your petals scattered into the scrub,

and still I curse our short season.

SHIPWRECK

In the end, it was a bestiary,
            a series of fantastic animals
                  you brought to the house:

tarantulas, ferrets, corn snakes,
            boa constrictor, sugar glider
                  you called Satan, and his mate

with huge eyes that shrieked
             like a drunk in rehab, and dove
                  into a paper cup for cover.

Gekkos, a hedgehog, a Gila monster
            that banged his tail against the cage
                  until it broke.

A few ran free, some escaped,
            others died. You brought in
                  every fearful creature

that moved, scurried, hid,
            a flailing Noah's Ark
                  that sank.

Your mother's hulk
            sunk under the sea,
                  wasn't enough.

Lisa Fleck Dondiego

YOU WERE GONE BEFORE

they pushed you through
        the emergency room doors.

I'd mistaken the skulls
        on your T-shirts,
                the skeleton mask you wore

that Halloween
        when you kissed me,
                for ordinary bluffs.

Touching the spot on the rug
        where they'd tried
                to jolt you alive,

I blanked out,
        conjured instead our first dance
                when you pressed into me,

like your bonsai whose trunks
        when they touched
                intertwined.

At the wake, I kissed
        your red beard,
                slipped a note in your pocket:

Wait for me.

THINGS DISCOVERED LATER

The roll of film
at the developers, a photo

of your boa, Merlin,
wrapped around your neck.

Garden tools we used together,
gathering rust.

A tape of a quarrel,
keys lost in a drawer.

A journal from rehab
that stops mid-sentence.

Little bottles thrown in the woods,
a trail of crumbs.

The power gone black
at midnight.

Sounds of trees cracking
like icebergs—electricity sputters—

candles lighted by my daughter—
your absence a darkness

I can touch.
I pray for help.

Snow-laden, the birch
bends to lift the lantern

from its post,
like many years before

when it had hung suspended
from the branch until

one still
spring morning,

it crashed onto the walk,
splintered.

Wiser this time,
I cut it loose.

I did not die, it says.
I did not die.

ROCKABYE

I told myself the drink
        wasn't going to take
                a toll. The cradle

held fast in the treetop
        whenever the wind blew. Who knew
                the bough would break,

we'd both awaken,
        rocked by your shaking,
                fall to the ground?

Too long lulled, the childish
        song ended, I kneel on the hardness
                of your new grave.

PRAYERS

You would have hated those Mass cards
piling up on the table from friends
and family, praying for blessed peace
in perpetuity. How many infinities
can you live through? The sins were
anyway not yours, belonged to others.
Even if the mourners meant well,
Holy fruit of Mass six times a day
was against your religion of sarcasm.
I'm sure you're laughing now
in your coffin. I know prayers said over
and over will never bring you back.

YOU LIVE NOW

on the mugs, key chain,
on the tiny license plate your name
is printed on. In the tools you left
to clip the mammoth vines,
set up the Christmas tree,
put together my son's basketball stand,
my daughter's clothes cabinet,
my window boxes and arbor,
all with meticulous care.

Lisa Fleck Dondiego

LAMB

My daughter cried the way she did
when the lullaby in her raggedy lamb
fell silent, swore she saw you
sitting in the living room.

Merry Christmas, Kevin, she wrote in the snow
in wide circles with smiley faces and hearts
on the rear window of your broken-down
car, still in the driveway, because

you talked to her
about things that mattered—
wrote: *To my Adopted Daughter*,
crossed out *Adopted*.

In pictures with you, she stood close,
clasping her hands the way she did
when she was happy. My daughter
took the last photo.

It sits on her dresser
beside the frogs,
the heart-shaped boxes,
the broken lamb.

GOING FOR A WALK OVER THE BRIDGE AT THE TEATOWN NATURE CONSERVANCY

I walked around the lake
past the duck blind and boathouse
to a leafy trail

along the forested brook
where sunlight barely reached
to the spot

where in spring we had taken
all the pictures of each other
on the bridge

A winter storm
had washed it away
Through the trees

nothing but
the rush of water
over rocks, you gone too

No railing to hold
no place to cross
no way forward

Lisa Fleck Dondiego

TWO POEMS
JILL EVANS

ON LEAVING HOME

It takes forever. And still
you never get there.
It is a destination, this
leave-taking,
a deep sky you cross under
beneath the unknown.

It is an intractable breath
echoing your first newborn cry
or the willowy sigh of a spring storm
in the wide open changes
of everything,
when your mother and father are busy,
their eyes turned away. You go on
beginning.

You take with you
all you can bear:
your reputation,
your old habits,
all your unease heaped inside you
like old unfolded clothes. You stockpile
miscellaneous flatteries, back-up plans
for an understudy to love you,
other maps of the self.

You bring caution with you
like a compass. You carry
your old opinions held rigid
as unbending postures
tensed against the wind.
You hoard sugary daydreams entwined
in the sheerest garments of time.
You send out flares
made of shiny words. Like these.

And you wonder if
you will fall from far away.
And just who
you will turn into
when you do.

TALKING TO TIME

Hush, time. Be still. Cling to me.
Grab my past and pull
with all your might.

Hug me forward, slow
and confident as rain on water.
Become a frozen sunset,

a heart-shaped galaxy expanded,
unfading as the speed of light.
Don't be so eager to get going.

Let me boss you around. Let me
take you for granted, let me forget how much
you count with your endless start and stop.

Quit measuring everything, quit
eavesdropping on my body.
just glide. Remember later.

Keep someday ajar.
Be home waiting
at the entrance to my hopes.

Don't move a moment.
Steady yourself inside.
Be gathered there intimate

as breath, invisible as wisdom, fierce
as your power over all
that sprawling life you shoulder.

Hold my naked heat inside
your embrace. Hug my homeless reach
inside your grasp.

Your rules are translucent shards
of nothing I can fathom. You are all
there is of possibility.

No matter matters more.
Remain bottomless,
my unbroken vessel. Contain me

more and more. Stay fast
on my side. Let me become more
of me. Hang onto me.

And I
will bear
the rest.

POEMS

JOHN GREY

END OF THE DAY

Being human,
you inherited
the bark of your parent's insides.

Pain flowing, body bending, yes, suffering is still here.
All of its mangy tigers and coiling snakes.
You leave yourself so open. No wonder they find you.
Bright-lit afternoons, Sunday dinners and sunflowers
rising and bursting - refuse to acknowledge their
significance.

The sunlight falls just so -shadowy demise,
star-crossed downfalls,
and good hunting for whatever's inside you.

MAKING A NIGHT OF IT

The trees have been swallowed,
the sky likewise
leaving just these twinkling golden holes.
The earth,
robbed of eyes,
relies on the clip of foot on pavement,
the touch of what could only be a fence post,
for its existence.
Without me opening the gate
and strolling the path up to your door,
it is just a lump of earth and rock
rolling through space.
And then I knock,
a light goes on in your house somewhere.
You're setting up an alternate planet.
I step inside.
Sorry Earth, but that's the end of it.

John Grey

FUNERAL OF A LESSER MORTAL

Chance remark flung me back
fifty years first funeral second hand tears
an Aunt's funeral the one who patted my head
it was the funeral of a hand then brief contact
lowered into the ground dirt tossed
atop an occasional unwanted kiss on the cheek
and family members gathered around
saying goodbye to the unneeded the uncalled for
maybe the telephone conversation they thought
would never end or the muffins hard as rocks
or the gossip that proved to have no foundation
their cheeks wet and red lesson number fifty seven
all is forgiven when someone dies
another chance remark pulls me free of
this cold gray ceremony back into the present
death of a movie star one of my favorites
loved him in.... should have won the Oscar for..
made me think aunts never star in anything
or at least whatever roles they play are limited
to brief contacts with protesting little boys
surely once my aunt must have made love to my
uncle but I never saw that film and at the end
dead as a coat rack neither did she

WHERE DID THEY GO?

Abandoned buildings
are deader than the ground,
than the granite hills,
the tree-less mountains.
A scouting party
through dusty laboratories,
rusty machinery,
dilapidated living quarters
is a funeral
with rooms for corpse.
You want to tap into
the fragile thoughts of ghosts,
then read the diaries,
load the disk drives,
rub the scratching on the walls.
No shock, no shudder,
to a death in wasteland.
But when humanity surrounds itself
with such familiar trappings
and still perishes,
how secure then are the ones
who tread so warily among the missing?
Atop a disheveled bunk,
I find a photograph of a woman,
signed "To Frank, love Jane."
Ah Frank, you are my eyes,
lowered like coffin lids.
Jane, you are my memory,
 smiling a floral wreath.

DRIPPING POEM

Long steamy shower,
water dripping down my skin.
Rain's abated
but it's still dripping from the eaves.
Leaky pen when signing check -
ink dripping on my name and address.
Another paper cut,
blood dripping on the blank sheet
that did this to me.
Rotted washer - tap's dripping.
Old man reckons he's done pissing
but not quite -
urine's dripping down his underwear.
Gale lights the candles -
wax is dripping.
The pan on the stove overflows -
gravy's dripping to the linoleum floor.
Sore on my arm -
pus dripping.
Old man at the kitchen table -
saliva dripping down his chin.
End of the day,
shadows dripping -
no, they kind of ease their way in.
The dark overall
is more an encumbrance,
not something that stains the light
a drop at a time.
We watch TV,
cuddle each other
but no liquid escapes.
The old man snores
but keeps his fluids to himself.
We've almost made it to sleep

without another drop.
But then, in bed,
I tell her a sad thing I heard today.
Her eyes moisten -
tears are dripping down her cheeks.
"It's okay dear," I tell her
in my sympathetic, caring voice
saved for such occasions.
Direct from my smarmy tongue -
drip, drip, drip.

THE LOVER
JOE MURPHY

The Lover

1.

I won't lean upon your leafless branches.

The ice on my forehead is melting.
The first green shoot
thrusts from my chest.

Soon, buds will grow from my fingertips;
birds nest within my dreams.

2.

I can't remain a seed
until the seasons change.
I'll break frozen ground to reach you.

I've kicked aside a bottle
filled with messages
I was too frightened to send;

tossed off a mask
that fell over my eyes,
causing me to stumble
into the arms of strangers.

ONLY THE MEMORIES COUNT
COLLEEN POWDERLY

Even to Cry

My last boyfriend thought he could control it
but before he thought twice he stole mouthwash
shoved its long neck down past the gag reflex   swallowed
        brutal draughts

He lied to everyone of course
sold a denim trucker's jacket I gave him as a gift
left his backpack on the bus
went to school drunk got thrown out of class   lied   lied
            to everyone
most the girlfriend who'd bet the house on his sobriety

Fell one night in front of my building   passersby asking if
            he were sick   face down in that year's geraniums
black mulch chips pushing into his skin
crazy-quilt lines on his cheek
black specks on his forehead when he came to   braced his
          back against a tree   pulled a pint of Four Roses
          from his bag

After that night no limits
till a theft caught on camera took him to jail
He thought he'd catch a break because he couldn't remember
He thought he'd catch a break because he was a student
& the laptop he stole was from a TA on campus
He thought they'd slap his wrist not make him pay for it
He had papers to write & he needed more time
He thought he'd be excused   another chance   he'd get
          more time
That's just what they decreed   1 & 1/2 to 3 medium security
not even a hug before he left

What would I say to him if I could?
how I got through it on my knees?
how I begged the hurt to end?
hid in bed but couldn't sleep?

one long winter drove to work in the dark   banker's lamp
          the only light in my office
focused on the work—the contracts—the language
phone calls from peers who told unfunny jokes
heart swelling deflating inside me

back home in the dark
escaped to my little room
lay dressed *even in shoes* on my side facing the TV
MASH episodes seen so many times   *several with him*
outcome known when the first frame glowed

awake at 3 a.m. for *Star Trek*   up at 4 a.m. to work again
time moving only on the job   weekends a full month long

How to explain it?   I gave what was in me?   one last try
          at love?
trial-by-fire of trust I'd tried for years?

Colleen Powderly   230

Dreams I'd formed once he'd finish his degree
both working   no children
quiet homelife   cooking together
he the better chef so I'd wash dishes
movies together   shopping together
loving together

everyday pleasures & simple life I'd settle for grateful for love
          at last
gone with a bottle of mouthwash   six-pack of beer   or
          whiskey he could steal
gone down a silent tributary when he went off to jail

He made no contact while *MASH* episodes ran   neither
          voice nor letter
I left scraps of self-respect on my pillow with my sweat
unable   finally   even to cry

The Art Museum at the End of the World

That night in dreams I am outside the art museum at the end
          of the world   the Thinker greets me beside the
          walk where my feet don't hurt

Further on the David towers over me   the breadth of his
          chest a wonder   his delicate genitals & long-
          muscled thighs a spell in white marble centuries old

Glass doors are garlanded by full-petaled flowers
          peonies—roses—my favorite wind-bent daisies
          chiseled gingerly

sunlight falls on them—delineates shadows—extends details
          I think they're moving   I'm light-headed but keep
          my balance
drift through the spell-opened doors to find Mona Lisa
          smiling

In the front rooms Renoirs shine their dazzling blues   I
          wander his walls   the love in his portraits   Two
          Sisters I saw in Chicago revisited now that there's
          time

Manets are next   his haunting darkness   blacks
          separated from blacks from near-blacks from
          whites—gallery lights chiseling each shade

I hear a whisper behind me   turn to galleries of Van Goghs
          the ones I never saw except flattened in books—
          sketches—studies—a single iris
field of irises   field of wheat   The Sower   The Potato
          Eaters grim & blatant
sketch of a sunflower   Sunflowers lighting its own room

A whisper rises behind me   I turn—find the works from
        Chicago
The Drinkers blue-&-white uniforms beneath clouds
        impasted thickly with white
 Fishing in Spring with its startling pinks
then The Poet's Garden & I'm crying as I did in life when I
        saw wind move its leaves & thought I might touch
        them
I want to walk that garden now

The voices rise   there are almost words
I leave my Van Goghs follow human cadence to the room
        where one painting hangs

Main Street Bridge, Rochester, 1908
the buildings over the Genesee
laundry hanging above the bowed windows of a tea room
walls shadowing windows where light never shines

The voices come as if through fog   directionless   half
        heard

they're from souls trapped above the tea room smelling cakes
        while garlicky stews waft out on the wind from their
        rooms
I smell their wanting cakes & china from that other world

We're together above a noiseless river as their voices float on
        the wind
I hear the lilt of their anger   the cacophony of their desires

The Chair Rider

It's November

the killing frost was weeks ago & few leaves wait to fall
from the drying limbs of winter-ready trees

Trees   their movements in wind
I see out the permanently dirty windows of my studio
         apartment

Afternoons the nursing home across the street releases a
         resident
who rides up & down the sidewalk in her motorized chair
carefully smoking   adhering to all littering laws
but prey nonetheless to addiction
unable   *likely unwilling*   to give up a source of immense
         pleasure
I would make a world in which such simple pleasures were nonlethal

***

February finally gone with its killing lack of sun
March changes welcome   I want the time change to
         extend my days
the only good thing Ronald Reagan ever did

I watch for changes in willow withes—first harbinger of my
         spring
outside my window maple branches reach desperately for sun
         still hiding behind clouds

but willow withes by the interstate have quickened with pale
         green
not long now   *patience   patience*

Colleen Powderly

Cigarette in hand Chair Rider patrols the sidewalk beneath
          crisscrossing locust branches

I feel fondness though we've never met
dark blue jacket   hood pulled over head
features indistinguishable as she trundles corner to corner
stops to watch cars cross the intersection at the edge of her
          world
watch people move off to wider-painted lives than she may
          have ever known

than either she or I will know again

***

2 weeks after Easter I wait for the spirit of celebration
resurrection   new spring
but I am wordless
try to force writing   begin the flow again

In the afternoon Chair Rider patrols her sidewalk
cigarette hanging from her mouth—hand on her chair control
I watch her pull in smoke with one side of her mouth
blow it out the other
she disappears around a corner

2 minutes later she's back   stops   in slow motion
          raises her hand to the butt
by degrees of pain lowers her arm past her blue-blanketed
          legs   drops the butt on still-wet ground
pulls her arm back—lets it fall when her hand is over the
          switch
rides up the driveway to her door

The sky is very blue   it is seasonably warm   her
movements are slower—stiffer
Is this her last spring?

SOME POEMS
WILLY PRIMEAU

1

Your power lies deep inside. To keep it sometimes hard. The world around can steal from you. It can suck your power dry. The battle ebbs and flows. The struggle hauntingly real. Each moment is a test. Your need to battle is on. You cannot change the force. Their powers are for real. You power though its wains sometimes. Is truly there to stay. So, latch on to your energy source. It's there to lift you up. Believe in your inner strength. It's what makes you who you are. You are the one true you. It's in you to fight on. So, grab your guts and fight. Your stronger than you know. Win back your self-esteem. Always remember that the world loves you just the way you are.

2

The pain is real.
The anguish there.
From whence it came ... I do not care.
Each day it grows... So deep inside.
From its control... I struggle to hide.
It's power so strong... There's little recourse.
It's stronger than me... It's such a force.
I seek to hide.... From its control.
As I quickly fall... Into its arms.
The will to fight.... Can dwindle fast.
As on each day... My gas runs dry.
But fight I will... To win back strength.
The strength it takes... To fight for air.
The air I need... To carry on.
So, let it be known... That I am here.
The push is there.... The flame is on.
From where I got it... I do not care.
For I am here... to fight for strength.
The strength I need... to carry on.
So, watch out fear... My light is on.
It's my turn now.

The end is near.
I fear the ghost.
The end is near.
I fear it most.
The end is near.
My fear it grows.
The end is near.
Am I the ghost?
The end is near.
I'm hot then cold.
The end is near.
As I grow old.
The end is near.
It's who I am.
The end is near.
It's vivid now.
The end is near.
The time is passing.
The end is near.
It's flashing by.
The end is near.
All is settled now.
The end is here.
I am the ghost.

The fear is there... The pain is real... from where I'll turn, I do not know. From hence it came I can only surmise... for my inner sole is lost in time. Believe me when I shout in anguish... this turmoil has a hold on me. Its grip is solid and ever so strong... to shake myself free seems like a dream. The struggle so real the anguish consuming. My world is spinning... spinning out of control. Please help me when I am shaking and lost. Your gentle nature makes it all seem worthwhile. A hug... a wink or your marvellous smile will always turn my life around... at least for now.

My world is comforting, nourishing and wet. The universe is forever in a constant flowing and all-encompassing state. My world although restricting feeds me all the nourishments... comfort... love... and support that I will need to push forward into a fast paced and awe-inspiring world. Development and growth are who I am. My vision is limited... my movement varies and I search for answers on how to manoeuvre through the fluids of my encasement. My size... my growth... and my development are all factors that determine my fate. To grow too slow or too quickly can be my demise. My control is limited... my outcome can vary depending on factors that are out of my control. Everything about me depends on so many factors... and yet I have so little control. I Grow... I Experience... I Am. Everything is moving so fast. Everything is forever changing. Everything is working towards that day that my Bubble bursts and I Truly Am.

5 POEMS
RUTH SABATH ROSENTHAL

Every Last Bit of Sale Yarn

Sad but true, I'd never seen my cousins wearing
the sweaters our maiden Aunt Minna knitted
for each one of them (me too, & guilty too)
though we'd heartily thanked her, praised her,
held her creations against ourselves so Auntie
could admire her handiwork, in the flesh, so to
speak: argyle crewnecks; raglan-sleeve cardigans —

all made of sale yarn to fit her budget. Sale yarn
that proved too heavy for those slim framed among us
& too flimsy for the broad. & to boot, oh the colors
she picked to knit, irregardless of our skin tones:

shades of brown & puce, neon orange & chartreuse —
no one ever asking her to alter her future choice of yarn
color & weight, or her particular measuring technique.
On the contrary, we kept rewarding Auntie with love &
attention each time we received one of her knitted wonders.

& so, Auntie kept knitting on & on, her bone needles
clicking & clacking their way to the end of each row
of sale yarn, thus, pin-pointing her knack for growing
the sweaters into less & less of what we needed, wanted.

Then, one Christmas, we, cousins, announced en masse,
after fortifying ourselves with a good amount of cousin-
laced eggnog, that "We don't need any more sweaters
since we've stopped growing & the last sweaters
you made us fit well" &, also, something to the effect of:
We've grown really fond of shopping lately, especially
for winter hats, scarves, mittens and gloves.

Auntie literally took what we had to say to heart
& thus turned her creative efforts to crocheting. More
sale yarn, but now crocheted into cartons-full of
4" squares she then fabricated into one bed-throw
after another, until our households ran out of beds.
What followed those throws was the last of her
creations: pompom tassels for tying on luggage,
which afforded her the use of every last bit of
yarn in her possession.

To this day, the eye-popping beauties may be seen
adorning a select group of suitcases that ride round
airport carousels, or stream through a throng
of travelers at given anytime, anywhere.

A Poet, Past Tense. Present Tense, What?

I'd brought her a journal—
fabric covered
with a plethora of pink roses
on a burgundy background
hard-bound
within that
blank lined pages
she'd have filled with verse
to her heart's content if only
that brain of hers hadn't been
wracked with indignities
wreaked on it
thus limiting her to
filling the first few pages
only
filling them with a smattering
of partial words
then interspersed
among blank pages
a few pages
with sparse groups of letters
hap-hazard throughout
a stretch of several pages
& further on
past more blank pages
more letters strung together
with those ending in
scrawls trailing off
in-
    to
       the
          tiniest
             scribble

Unrelenting Till the End of Time

bleed! burn!
the devil's deeds
decreed
an Anti-Christ
& hoards of his
man-killing sheep
nonstop
murder millions
sinew & flesh rot
flesh & bone burn to ash
indeed
the blind man sees all
blood curdling!
screams! bleats!
indeed
the shepherd hears it all
while
across the sea
farther than
the eye would see
mankind sleeps
a gracious slumber
round the clock
like the good shepherd
& his ardent flock
as sinew & flesh rot
flesh & bone burn to ash
nonstop
flesh & bone to burn
to ash & bone
till time in memoriam

A House Not a Home

the house still
but for fierce currents
of indifference
charging through
narrow corridors
and stairs winding
round and round
the mausoleum
father mother sister brother
each dead set
against ending up
anywhere
near one another
even accidentally

my mother's in the hospital

her infirmity
ever threatening
her capacity
to recognize me
i pray
she'll have the clarity
to convey
she's okay
with dying
i pray
she'll get to soar
the stratosphere —
a winged soul
with angels
guiding her
to that pasture
where flowers
are blooming
year round
beyond
rationale
that this
could happen
lifts me to smile
visit to visit
none-the-less —
this visit
mother's in
& out of
where
one goes in
the throes of
leaving their body
then

Ruth Sabath Rosenthal

she murmurs
mommy
& is gone —
gone into
the beam
of light in which
i wish
to believe she'd seen
her mother
beckon her to

The Writers Circle 2

HOW TO MEASURE TIME
VERA SALTER

HOW TO MEASURE TIME

On this date I have lived one month longer than my mother

The earth is 4.54 billion years old

He made coffee at 6.40 in the evening because he thought it
was morning

The Long Now Clock ticks once a year
and the cuckoo comes out on the millennium

Mouthless moth larvae feed on wallaby grass for two years
and metamorphose to seek sex and starve in four days

Prufrock measured out his life in coffee spoons

Seventeen-year cicadas emerge on time for their few weeks
of life

You were pushed into a long white crypt after eighty-three
years

END OF TIMES
GERARD SARNAT

ON THE SAME WAVELENGTH

i. While Family Flowers On Mother's Day, 2019

Five grandsons and counting --
the youngest boy carries a bouquet
of wild blossoms (oy they preferred
such even though cut/ destroyed flora appear
strictly verboten under Jewish law) for you
my atheist parents as I visit their graveside
very first time since Mom joined Dad.

Just up one hill from their relatively new plots,
equidistant between them plus where half-century
wife's disa.pproving Orthodox parents reside
(who likely are plotzing looking down
annoyed from more mature burial sites)
-- we now decide to visit our own plots
which will house us too soon enough.

ii. first time to die
-- thanks to PBS *Frontline's* 30April2019 "The Last Survivors"

bird chirps above Auschwitz.
ultimate cognitive dissonance.

industrial strength genocide,
which flame is my mother's?

74 years later, I show grandkids
the family scroll in which those

who perished, noted by Stars
of David, form a starry sky.

iii. On The Same Wavelength haiku

Is passed parents love
∞ graveside
visit λ?

Mesmerized By My Entomologist Son's Story

-- thanks to *Pulpmouth*

You make eye contact with a complete and utter stranger
with a tripartite exoskeleton and elbowed antennae
nodding from an odd head containing five compound eyes.

Titanic Promethean fire ants steal flawed flames
from life breathers, playing trickster
deities plumbing soulful sacrificial terror dream depths.

Paper wasps gathers fibers of the passed,
then construct nests
out of commensurate pulp plus saliva.

Late at night, you can hear them at work:
theirs is a labor
communing with another side.

Hives investigate thin partitions
between living and dead
following gut punch intuition.

This leads beyond rich arras tapestry
into disembodied rooms
where psychogeography meets static electricity.

Magnetism happens when we sense
body pulses standing behind us
which touch ink stains traced on wallpaper.

FOUR POEMS

ANN TAYLOR

Reaching Conclusions

Some endings etch in my mind –
graduations, retirements, deaths –
my last chat with Dad, he so happy
with his new metal detector,
my spaniel killed while I was at school
by a plumber's speeding pick-up,
my *Beowulf* class cut short
that sunny September morning.

But on some afternoon,
I gave up keying roller skates
onto my sneakers. On another,
I must have fought my last cap-pistol war.
One day, I shared a last outing
with Ma, Mary, Marie (and Me),
shorthanded in my diary to *M4*.
And one night, I'm sure I heard
my final banjo twang at the Hillbilly,
and at some point, mercifully
gave up my *Cripple Creek* lessons.

On a certain Sunday, I know
we crepe-papered our last kids'
birthday bash. Which Sunday?
Or was it Saturday? Which kid?

Library Demolition

To clear space for the *Learning Commons*,
    venue for new pedagogies and technologies,
bulbous black veins ripple.
    It heaves its heavy head
this way and that, rumbles rough,
    chooses a shaky spot to bite into –
toothful, fangful – to grind, shred,
    smoke puffing up over twisted spoils
stacking up and up. No one, even helmeted,
    dares the din.

Muncher isn't monstrous enough,
    Crane too feathery.
This *Wyrm* roars, reaches my old third-floor space –
    once cozy with soft chair,
wrap-around desk,
    shelves weighted with bound books.
The unblinking eye surveys the site,
    neck stretches up for the widest look-down
from above, blows open a hole through silt
    to cloud . . . and snorts.

Still Life

All my years growing up, she was the one
to awaken the house. Into her nineties,
she was dressed by sunrise for daily Mass.

She rarely rested, filling her later years
with the thrift shop, altar flowers,
Sunday school, music theater,
zoos with her grandchildren,
home-baked Danish, her favorite
Mermaid slots at Foxwoods.

I don't remember seeing her sleep,
until today as I approach her,
formal in her embroidered blouse,
cascades of flowers embracing her.

She looks so at peace, they say . . .
so pretty. But she and I resist this still life.

I expect her to rise up, announce,
*Let's get **out** of here!*
Cut flowers always remind me of funerals!

Ann Taylor

Disaster Tourism, Willey's Slide, 1826

By the hundreds – poets, painters, hikers, ghouls –
we come to re-live that night's wind,
to hear the torrent lashing the windows,
the Saco surging to the doorstep
of their small mountain inn,
six miles from everyone.

We imagine tall trees soldiering down
the black slope, toppling into cracked rock,
a rush of thick mud.

We see the boulder outcrop,
like a neat parting of hair,
split the mudslide in two,
leave only their house untouched,
suffer with Polly, Sam, five children,
two hired hands, as they rush outdoors
to what seems a shelter,
all crushed by the cascade,

We grieve with rescuers
unearthing bodies only for re-burial.

Through dimmed windows,
we spy Sam's potbelly stove,
beds turned down, Polly's *Bible* open,
white candles guttered out.

With some guilt, gratitude, pride even,
we seek messages here,
but when evening wind snaps
at the firs above us, our gloom diverts
to the story of the family dog
rescued safe alone inside – hungry, ecstatic.

A bracing dose of disaster, the pamphlets promise.

(19th century tourism, focusing on disaster sites)

UNSENT LETTERS:HIDDEN FEELINGS
BLAIR UROWITZ

The blame games(s)

The back and forth,

The constant
inconsistency,

That's what it's like—
you and me.

The blame games
that we play,
each one of us must
get our way.

Two hot heads and
two heavy hearts,

We ended faster
then we could start.

A resignation letter.

I am sorry
I can't come into work
Because my mind is
Controlling me,
I mean, not like
In the crazy way but
The normal kind, like
The type of people who's
Minds are too brilliant
To control, like
When you contain so much
Life in your soul that
You don't know how to shut off;

A job cannot keep
This mind contained,
I'm sorry
I can't come in,
I'm in pain.

(But like, the normal kind).

When will i

My legs run faster
Than my lungs can breathe,

Just tire them out.
Tire them out.
Make them too tired
To control me,

I sprint my young legs
Around the room,

Thoughts pacing faster
Than Usain can run,

I can't keep up.

I drive my legs into
The kitchen,

Nails deep into
my skin,
When will
this end?
When will I
 begin?

The call

Vibrations ringing,
She picks up the phone.
A few words spoken,
A sad look shown.

What seems like tomorrow,
Is already past—
And that, just a memory,
A sad song, at best.

Her anger rises
On my touch,
I cannot help but
Love you too much.

Pain
From a life,
Now done,

Even though yours
Has just begun.

I love you, I do,
But my love can't
Heal you,
From a life once lived,
Now buried.

My love is not
Enough for you.

Distance

Could feel like an end,
If you do not take care,
Of the relationship you share,
With another person.

That's how it was
With you and me,
We couldn't see
What was more important,

The guilt or the dream,
The dream of you and me,
Of what could be,

But we were left
With silence,
And our wounds were left
unhealed;

Time does that
To distance,

But what's real?

A mother, called a sister.

I grew up with you
Under my wing,

A mother, called a sister,
I always did everything
For your sake,

I feel so selfish
Leaving you,
The miles between us
Grew,

So fast and
So far,

I miss you, my kings
I still sing
To you,
In my dreams,

I wish it wasn't
How it could be,

I know you'll get through this,
I feel selfish
For moving,
For leaving you,

But its how it had
To be,

One day
Well be closer,
One day, you'll see.

Blair Urowitz

Renew us.

Our minds
Cannot disconnect,

Our hearts were always
In respect
To how hard
We feel,

But we never knew
What's real.

I couldn't disguise
The pain from your eyes,
To what love felt like
In my past lives,

And it tasted so good,
On your lips,
I almost miss
The sting you left.

But then your pain grew,
With every word I spoke
To you,

We are not well
For each other,

From then on, I knew
That we have expired,

Both left with a bruise.

NONFICTION

GRANDMA AND GRANDPA'S BUNGALOW
MERYL BAER

As I drive into the mountains I quickly discover the once pristine Catskill Mountain landscape is no longer unspoiled. Billboards urge travelers to detour and stop by gas stations and convenience stores, restaurants and retailers. The sights from the highway - auto repair shops, junkyards and run-down buildings - detract from the area's allure.

My destination is Joyland Road.

Joyland Road is etched in my memory. Joyland is summers in the mountains, lengthy days playing with seasonal friends, card games and Mah Jongg with Grandma, my sister and assorted visitors. Joyland is the summer with Smokey, our dog, and the summer my cousin almost drowned in the lake. Joyland is idyllic childhood summers remembered, whether or not they were actually perfect.

A marked exit off the highway makes it incredibly easy to

find Joyland Road. Turning onto the two-lane potholed street, I pass deserted bungalow colonies, crumbling wood cabins, houses occupied but in disrepair, and abandoned businesses.

Then I see Grandma and Grandpa's country estate. The two bungalows sit silent and deserted behind a patchy brown lawn. No towering shade trees block the view, only stumps where once-majestic branches provided shade during hot summer afternoons. A garage, rundown since I was a kid, completes the picture.

Is the property permanently abandoned or only uninhabited during the winter? It is hard to tell. Perhaps the owners will drive up sometime in May or June, turn in the dirt driveway, jump out of their van and unpack a summer's worth of provisions. The lawn will turn green and newly planted flowers bloom. Outdoor chairs and a table will fill the yard and fresh paint brighten the dingy white shingles.

I stand on the gravel walkway and envision the long-ago. I hear echoes of two little girls' rowdy voices as they race around the yard. Grandma calls the girls to lunch. In the far corner of the property, Grandpa hunches over his vegetable garden. A car careens too fast down Joyland Road. A neighbor walks by and hollers, "Hello! Anybody home?"

***

Grandpa's car made its way along the narrow road, rutted

from harsh winter weather and neglect, passing bungalow colonies with one and two-room cabins, a swimming pool, community hall, a laundry shed. A handful of dilapidated farmhouses, partially concealed behind peeling fences and overgrown shrubbery, also dot the landscape.

Rounding a curve Grandma and Grandpa's two cottages came into view. Anchored on concrete blocks, boasting white shingles with red trim, the square one-story structures eagerly awaited their young summer occupants. The smaller bungalow rented out each summer. My grandparents, my sister and I resided in the larger house all summer. But it was not large. In fact, it was not sizable at all.

The car slowed, passed a mailbox and turned into the dirt driveway, skirting a hand-painted white wooden sign proudly displaying the name 'Mer-Jan', the impressive designation for this summer haven, named after Meryl and Janice – me and my sister. We spent long, lazy 1950s summers here. Grandpa drove to our house on Long Island on the last day of school and transported us to his mountain sanctuary. We stayed until Labor Day.

A multi-purpose room encompassing the length of the house greeted folks entering the cabin through the only en-trance, the front door. A black and white TV sat at one end and a table and chairs at the other end. Well-worn upholstered chairs, a sofa, coffee table and an end table or two completed the furnishings. Directly across from the entrance, nestled in the middle of a small hallway, sat the bathroom. A bedroom anchored each side of the hall, small rooms consumed by a couple of twin beds.

The kitchen, located opposite the TV in the main room, was hidden behind a paneled wall. I don't remember the space – I obviously did not spend much time there, an area adequate for Grandma to prepare three meals a day but offering no extra space for kids to linger.

Breakfast miraculously appeared at 8:00 a.m., lunch at noon and dinner at 6:00 p.m., a pattern established years earlier when Grandpa owned a store below their apartment in Queens, New York. He would eat breakfast, go downstairs and open for business. At noon he returned to the apartment, lunch on the table. He worked in the store all afternoon, closed at 6:00 and walked upstairs for dinner, a hot meal waiting for him.

A garage with green weather-beaten shingles and two massive wooden doors sat at the end of the driveway. Grandma kept a freezer inside stocked with homemade foods. Opening the freezer door with one hand and holding it up, Grandma rummaged around with her free hand in the ice-cold interior, searching for a specific labeled item. I am sure carefully wrapped packages remained on the bottom of the freezer for years, growing ice coatings and eventually discarded by subsequent owners. Garden tools, lawn chairs, a bridge table, discarded furniture and assorted cast-off objects filled the rest of the garage. No car ever graced the inside of the building as far as I know.

Woods surrounded three sides of the property. Only one other house could be viewed from the yard, a two-story farm-house across the street. Overgrown grass and weeds – mainly weeds - surrounded the run-down house. I never saw a car in the driveway and never noticed any occupants.

Once or twice a summer Grandma, my sister and I walked about two miles to the end of Joyland Road, where the fancy Concord Hotel dominated the countryside. Cars and people rushed everywhere, people dressed in golf and tennis attire scurried about, and folks sunbathed on lounge chairs in the enormous pool area. Kids shouted, scooted about, and sat on grassy knolls eating ice cream. I remember walking around the hotel lobby, a huge, bright space with faux-crystal chandeliers and plush chairs. Lines of people, suitcases in tow, waited to check in or out.

My grandmother, my sister and I walked down the road in the opposite direction from the Concord to a farm to buy eggs. Grandma Rose limped but walked long distances; at least the length seemed far to me at the time.

We walked to the bungalow colony next door to go swimming and play with friends.

We drove into town, purchased groceries, enjoyed lunch at the deli, indulging in corned beef and pastrami sandwiches, and went to the library, taking a long time choosing the perfect books to read while sitting in the hammock or rocking chair during the hottest part of the day.

We helped Grandpa in his vegetable garden and picked blueberries from bushes growing wild next to the house. Actually, I rarely strode into Grandpa's domain. Looking back I think he wanted his garden time to be his quiet interlude.

Evenings we played gin rummy and gorged on ice cream, a routine that inch by inch increased my waistline. Every night Grandpa also devoured a frozen Milky Way.

***

I had not laid eyes on the bungalow since the 1960s. As my sister and I left our single-digit years and advanced to life in our teens, we wanted to spend more time with friends at home on Long Island. Fleeting weekends replaced weeks in the country. By my senior year of high school Grandma's illness prevented her from spending time on Joyland Road. In March 1969, my freshman year in college, Grandma Rose died of breast cancer. Grandpa sold his beloved mountain retreat the following year.

MEMORARE
CHRISTINE CORRIGAN

Our mother-in-law left her apartment in the assisted living facility where she'd lived for the last three years with her aide guiding her to a waiting car. The family had organized several hours of outings and errands for her so Lina, my sister-in-law, and I could begin to clean, sort, and sift through her belongings before she moved to a "memory care" facility that provided the specialized care for Alzheimer's and dementia patients that she now needed.

Our mother-in-law's name is Regina Marie, but we've always called her Jeanne. Born in May, Mary's month, Jeanne's name is the Latin translation of Queen Mary, or to Catholics, Mary, Queen of Heaven. The Catholic tradition of naming a child after a saint is ancient. Indeed, St. John Chrysostom encouraged parents to choose for their children names of holy women and men, who were known for their strength and virtue to serve as role models. And, many consider St. Mary, the Blessed Virgin Mary, Mary Mother of God, or the Virgin Mary to be the greatest Christian saint.

memory: Origin Middle English, *memorie*, via Anglo-French, from Latin *memor*, "mindful," and akin to Greek, *mermera*, "care."

While we didn't speak of it, Lina and I were at Jeanne's apartment on that late May morning because no one else could face this task, neither Jeanne nor any of her five sons, including my husband, Tim, and Lina's husband, Kevin. Jeanne couldn't remember how to organize or sort anything. The weight of watching the slow loss of their mother's mind had crushed our husbands and their brothers, with Kevin fielding the regular calls from the facility about Jeanne's erratic and difficult behavior and Tim managing her lawyers, banking, and accountants. While Lina and I couldn't take those calls or handle her affairs, we could do this for them, for her.

Like Mnemosyne, the ancient Greek goddess of memory, we would be mindful in choosing what would go with Jeanne. We would take care that what mattered most would not be lost. We would hold the memories. Lina and I knew what Jeanne loved—photographs of Bob, her husband lost to cancer in 2013, her sisters, her children, and grandchildren, books (though she couldn't finish them anymore), journals and letters, her Bible, and favorite paintings and pictures of Paris, once her home. These were the things that mattered to Jeanne, and to us, our family, her love of words, stories, and writing, her lifetime of travels, and her deep, abiding faith. While we wanted her to have a comfortable chair for reading, a lamp, side table, and a bookshelf, we knew that her new apartment would be half the size of her current one. Much of the furniture, paintings, and collections of pottery and china, would go to a storage locker or be divided among the families when she moved. All of us would have something of hers and with that object, continue to hold a part of her.

I would ask for her desk and hoped that none of Tim's brothers would object. I wanted to have a place in my home to honor her with my words, a shrine of sorts to our shared love of writing, and where I'd keep my memories, my family photographs, journals, and letters.

Lina shouted, "Hey!" from the sweltering bedroom—the thermostat set high, though the day was bright and warm. My stomach lurched as I entered to find clothing piled, books stacked like bell towers, papers strewn, bags stuffed, and the bed layered with quilts and blankets.

We had several tasks: find Jeanne's jewelry, which could be hidden anywhere; locate the town's library books, which had gone missing; and make some sense of her belongings in advance of the move. Lina found the jewelry box, but she wasn't sure if all of the jewelry was in it. She searched Jeanne's closet, while I tackled the dresser.

I opened the top drawer and pulled out a stack of date-books, letters, postcards, and journals. Jeanne was religious in her use of agendas, calendars, and journals and a prolific correspondent. She carried notebooks and pens in her purse to write about where she traveled, what she read, the friends she visited, conversations overheard, or what the family did. I opened a datebook from 2011 and scanned the entries. She'd recorded all of the family's and her friends' birthdays and anniversaries as normal. On some days, Jeanne included notes,

"Book Club at OLF because of icy driveway at Nancy's. Snow late."

"Luncheon at library with Peg. Very delicious. Gina Berreca speaker. Very funny."

"To Italy." "Late day rain, electrical storm. Remained at Villa Margherita all day, reading in conservatory. Tea in late afternoon—brought on tray."

"Chris & Tim to Paris."

As I read Jeanne's notes, I could hear her words to me in phone calls and conversations during family meals or over cups of tea, snippets from the thirty-plus years I've known her.

I'm sending you a list of all the birthdays and anniversaries, so you'll remember to send cards.

Tell me, what are you reading? I'll send you Gina Berreca's book.

Remember to visit Sainte-Chapelle when you go to Paris. It's like the inside of a jewelry box.

I received the list of family milestones and assumed the task for years, although messages on Facebook and emails, more often than not, have replaced many of those cards. I enjoyed reading It's Not that I'm Bitter by Gina Berreca, an English professor at the University of Connecticut. Jeanne was right—Berreca was very funny. My family visited Sainte-Chapelle on our visit to Paris.

Sainte-Chapelle or "Holy Chapel" is located on the Île de la Cité and was built to house Louis IX's collection of holy relics, including the Crown of Thorns, said to be worn by Jesus

Christ during his passion and crucifixion. Sainte-Chapelle's lower chapel is dedicated to the Blessed Virgin Mary. A statue depicting Mary, crowned as Queen of Heaven—Regina Marie—with the Christ Child in her arms, stands at the chapel's entry.

relic: Origin Middle English, *relik*, via Anglo-French *relike*, from Latin, *relinquere*, "to leave behind."

I continued my slow search through the drawers. A single leather glove lay on top of little gift boxes, the kind that would contain a piece of jewelry. I opened one – three Hershey kisses, another – two grammar school photographs of a grandchild who was a sophomore in college. One held unmatched costume earrings. They looked like sea glass. I picked up a glove and found the silver bracelet that all of the grandchildren used for teething—snapped in two, a relic of long-ago days. I found photos of Bob, a stack of memorial cards from his funeral, and an envelope filled with Valentine's Day cards Jeanne and Bob exchanged. I quickly closed that envelope—those sentiments were meant only for them. I returned to Jeanne's date book because the past seemed a refuge from this present.

"Bob – Appointment at Memorial Sloan Kettering Cancer Center, Rockefeller Center."

"Thanksgiving at Tim & Chris's. Kevin and Lina drove Bob and me. Paul and Kelly with the children. A warm wonderful day."

I shut the date book. The end was beginning then, but no one knew it yet.

And memories of moments with her passed through my mind as I touched that which remained.

Remember a July morning on Cape Cod walking the beach, searching for sea glass?

Remember the drooling smiles, a child content in Jeanne's lap, holding that silver bracelet?

Remember Jeanne's instructions each year to use vinegar to wipe the bowl and whisk before making a meringue for the Thanksgiving lemon meringue pie?

I opened the next drawer, sorted through nightgowns and mismatched pajama pants, and unearthed a rubber spatula and a stack of mimeographed recipes, some written in French, with Jeanne's notes in perfect cursive. The stack contained over two years of recipes from cooking classes, sample menus, and lists for dinner parties featuring food that no one cooks anymore—French high cuisine.

"Look at these, Lina. They must be from when Jeanne took cooking classes at the Cordon Bleu when they lived in France. We need to scan and upload them to a Google drive so everyone can have access to them, just in case someone has a hankering for Canard aux Pruneaux," I said.

"What?" Lina asked.

"Duck with prunes. Get this. Step 1: 'Remove all feathers.' Can you imagine?"

Remember Jeanne told us she raced to her cooking classes in Paris after the boys left for school and spent hours at E. Dehillerin searching for the perfect pairing knife?

Remember the boeuf bourguignon Jeanne made, perfect on a cold, winter evening?

Lina and I laughed at the notion of plucking duck feathers then went on. She pulled old blankets from a chest, while I pushed aside socks and underwear and discovered another datebook. But the datebook from 2012 differed from 2011's. Gone were Jeanne's book group notes, comments about volunteer work, or visits with family. Bob's prostate cancer had returned in a fury and metastasized—first in his bones, then his lungs, and one long year later to his brain. She filled her days with appointments for Bob, consultations, and cancer treatments.

I put the book to the side when Lina whispered, "Oh, this."

She held a letter ripped in half she said she'd found under a brass and glass Christmas candleholder resting on a tabletop beneath the window.

"I think it's the list of missing books from the library, but I don't see these titles anywhere. Maybe she has them with her?" Lina asked.

I took the letter and noticed the date. It was from 2018.

"I doubt it. The letter is almost a year old. Why would she have hidden it? She must have been angry or embarrassed. I can't even guess."

"God. Look at this," Lina said as she passed me a list that she found near the library letter.

Grocies

Pre-cooked meat in packages

Tissues in all sizes

Special cheeses

Sanity pads. . . .

"Jesus. I could use some sanity pads right now," I said rubbing my temples as I looked out over the sunny parking lot.

"Me too. I'm going to take some of these bags down to the trash room," Lina said. Perhaps, she, like me, needed a moment. Jeanne often called me the daughter of her heart. After years of tumult with my own mother, my relationship with Jeanne had been easy—no accusations that I didn't understand her, no stormy late-night phone calls ending with "bitch" and a click, and no chance to tell her that despite it all I loved her, as my mom died suddenly when I was thousands of miles away. And now, I couldn't share more than small talk with Jeanne, as her mind wandered, her thoughts replaced with nervous laughter or her mutterings, "That's it." or "Okay, okay." I couldn't reconcile my memory of Jeanne and the living ghost of her former self.

How can it be that this woman—of words, stories, books, letters, grace, and faith—is losing her beautiful mind and her lifetime of memories? Does she even know?

Jeanne reminded us to pray "often." So, I did. As my tears fell, I prayed the Memorare:

Remember, O most gracious Virgin Mary that never was it known that anyone who fled to thy protection, implored thy help, or sought thy intercession was left unaided. Inspired with this confidence, I fly to thee, O Virgin of virgins, my Mother; to thee do I come;

before thee I stand, sinful and sorrowful. O Mother of the Word Incarnate, despise not my petitions, but in thy mercy hear and answer me.

Lina returned. Glancing at her watch, she said, "Jeanne's going to be back soon, and I have to get home to meet the girls after school."

"I need to get back to New Jersey before rush hour."

"We should take the rest of the trash out. I'll take the jewelry, so it doesn't get lost in the move," Lina said.

"That's fine. I'll take the paper – the recipes, journals, and letters, and sort through them."

We grabbed the bags, turned off the lights, and headed for the door, hoping our intrusion would go unnoticed. We passed a small table where a vase held, in fetid water, white oriental lilies, Jeanne's favorite flower. Faded, limp lily petals lay scattered across more papers and crumpled napkins. Tim and I had sent the lilies a week earlier for her birthday. They are the flower of May, a symbol of motherhood, virtue, and the Virgin Mary. As we left the apartment, her voice seemed to whisper to me,

Remember to cut the stamens from lilies, it makes them last longer.

remember: Origin Middle English, *remembren*, via Anglo-French from Late Latin *rememorari*, from Latin *re-*, "again or back," and *memorari*, "to be mindful of."

Remember to fill your minds, hearts, and lives with what matters.

Remember to care.

Remember to preserve the relics, those memories that remain.

Remember for Jeanne.

RAYS OF INSPIRATION
VICTORIA KLASSEN

In a place where the sun warms your skin, the gulls caw from above, the smell of salt drifts from the ocean, and the skies are painted with radiant streaks of colours, I met Ray Rolston.

At the time, I was an awkward pre-teen with braces and long hair. Nearly five times my age, Ray had beautiful, long dreadlocks and an easy smile. Ray was dressed in a tropical shirt as he introduced himself with a lively Caribbean accent and welcoming smile.

Art connected us.

Ray painted the beautiful Key West landscape where he lived—a world I only visited once a year. From a majestic pelican sitting by the ocean, to sunsets marbled with colours rarely captured, to iconic landmarks on the historic island, Ray created something for everyone. During the daily Sunset

Celebration at Mallory Square, you could always find Ray selling his prints and making new friends.

When I was older, studying writing at university, Ray asked me if I'd like to write a book about mermaids. We were sitting on the cobblestones outside my parents' vacation home after a seafood BBQ dinner. I had never written about mermaids, but I was excited to try. He sent me digital copies of his mermaid paintings for inspiration.

These paintings were my gateway to an underwater world filled with magic and mermaids.

A mermaid with a cobalt blue tail, equally blue eyes, and a fierce expression. A castle under the waves with towering white pillars and iridescent blue and pink peaks of mother-of-pearl. A smiling dolphin who was never far from the blue-tailed mermaid. Music bubbling up through the water, floating from the flutes of the mermaids.

These were the pictures I spent hours looking at, years dreaming about.

The story unfurled slowly but it took on a life of its own. At its centre, it was a story about how humans harm the environment and the oceans.

Back in Canada, as I wrote about the blue-eyed mermaid and her anger towards ocean-harming humans, Ray was also creating. He made new paintings featuring Hemingway's six-toed cats, sailboats tipping precariously in the angry ocean wind, and lobsters blissfully unaware of the humans with nets waiting to scoop them up.

When my parents first introduced me to Ray, he let me choose a small print to take home. I chose one of a baby manatee and a mother manatee side-by-side, floating peacefully in the water.

It was this painting that inspired the start of my story—the inciting incident.

As my story was taking shape, so was Ray's story. He published a book of his paintings, touched the lives of everyone he met at Sunset Celebration, and continued feeding the roosters that often wandered into his house.

In my early twenties, I was happy that Ray came to my mother's 50th birthday party in paradise. Amidst the dancing, games, and poolside dinner, Ray presented my mother with an original painting of a tropical Key West house with a sign that read "Casa Samantha."

A few days later, we visited his house for lunch. It was a colourful representation of who he was. Original paintings filled his walls from floor to ceiling. Half-finished canvases rested against each other in his bedroom. His place of creation was a stool and easel in his living room, speckled with paint.

Similarly, the chair and desk in my bedroom at home became my place of creation the following year as I completed a rough draft of my mermaid story. I had taken all of the ideas swimming around in my head and all of my notes scribbled on scraps of paper, and put them together. The blue-tailed mermaid had a name and a sister. The dolphin had a traumatic history. The manatees played an integral part in the story. And a stingray—Rolston the Ray—made some cameo appearances.

When I returned to the land of pelicans and mermaids the following year, Ray took me and my parents to a restaurant on Sunset Key. Our table was on the beach, close enough to hear the water lapping at the shore. The breeze rustled the palm leaves above and shaded us from the sun. I told Ray I had finished a draft of the mermaid story and that there was a stingray named after him.

Another year trickled by and I neared a quarter-century of life. I sat down, and worked on the story every day in the months leading up to my birthday. I edited, refined, and rewrote. I finished the story, a draft that I was proud to show to the world and to Ray. Little did I know, as I wrote the last few words of my story, Ray was enjoying the last few days of his story.

Ray never got to read my mermaid book, but he is the one who inspired it. He gave me a gift that no one else could—the gift of inspiration. I've spent days writing and years imagining an underwater world thanks to him. Ray brought the mermaids to life through his paintings, and I'm honoured that he trusted me to help tell their story.

Every evening, Ray enjoyed the breathtaking sunsets at Mallory Square. He often captured their beauty by painting them on canvases and sharing them with the world. Now the entire sky is his canvas.

In loving memory of Raymond Rolston, September 29, 1947- April 30, 2019.

THE OPEN ROAD AND AN OXYGEN TANK
NATHAN PRIMEAU

CLUNK

"Holy fuck, Grandma. These oxygen tanks are heavy," I let out as I caught my breath.

She had no sympathy for me. "Yeah, well be careful with them, will ya?"

Grandma got to wheel the tank that was currently filling her lungs on a nice convenient trolley. I, on the other hand, was stuck with lugging the two extra tanks to her car by hand. Let me tell you, oxygen tanks aren't light.

"Place them on the ground. Where your feet go," she told me.

I did as she told, and she thanked me before we crammed into her tiny white car.

We got on the road, to head out to my parents' campsite, and not long after leaving, grandma was up to her usual driving habits. We pulled up to our first stop, the intersection close to where my parents' and grandparents' road ended and a new one began. I still don't fully understand why a road changes name partway through.

For my grandma, it wasn't a stress-free stop. She, a mature and intelligent woman, spent a solid minute flipping off a driver in front of her and educating me on a list of curse words from her vocabulary. I guess that's what someone gets for driving too close to my grandma.

That moment embodies part of my grandma's unforgettable personality. I honestly used to believe that my grandma's cynicism and unapologetic humour were side effects of being on earth for too damn long. According to others, it turns out that she'd always kind of held that uniqueness to her.

The drive wasn't too long, between thirty minutes and an hour. Our topic of conversation centred on what it always did... which was me. Grandma wasn't as interested in herself, or even our destination. For nearly an hour, I had someone willing to make me the focus of her attention. She was good at it.

I didn't have a lot of people like that. Grandma was one of the very few people willing to show interest in what I was up to. It's one thing to ask someone, "How have you been?" These kinds of questions are commonplace. They lack depth. It's another thing to know the person deeply, ask more meaningful questions, and probe their mind to see how they're really feeling. How they've actually been. Grandma embodied this for me.

Something compelled me to remember that day, that drive. Somehow, it felt special, so I took out my phone and snapped a picture of the road in front of us. Of course, I'd post it on Instagram with a filter later.

This all happened in early August, and in less than a month I'd be in Ottawa starting school again. I thought that was the reason this trip felt so special. One last ride with grandma before I moved to another city. Instead, it just became the last ride.

She'd die roughly three months later.

Three months is all it took for my grandma to go from having the strength to drive, to losing her ability to breathe.

I didn't think about her dying anytime soon while I sat in her passenger seat. Hell, until I saw her for the first time with an oxygen tank, I thought she'd live forever. She could drive that car in her sleep, even when tubes were snaking their way out of her nostrils.

The mirage of her invincibility transcended beyond the car, and into the campsite. As I watched her talk to my mom, aunt, and the rest of the family. Everything about it felt so normal. Just like it did in the car. Just a bunch of people living in the present.

***

Time moved on, and so did I. I went to school, started studying, and even got a poem published in a small school magazine. Things felt pretty normal.

Slowly, I started to see that my mom was getting sadder. She wasn't joking like she used to. Like grandma used to. I just assumed my mom was fearing the worst.

I was gone at school. Mom couldn't bring herself to tell me the truth. Grandma wasn't okay, and she was slowly dying.

She didn't tell me that all of her organs would quit. That she was on oxygen because her lungs were already deciding to quit.

Mom knew that if I knew the truth, I would have packed up everything and spent every day I could with my grandma. Mom didn't want that, and grandma definitely didn't.

I can't help but think of all the times I could have spent time with my grandma. All the times I didn't want to just walk down the road, or go for a ride into town. She was close.

What I've got now is that low-resolution photo that I took on a whim.

ABOUT THE AUTHORS

Mackenzie T. Agard is many things including a writer, editor, artist, thinker, occasional yogi and novice kick boxer. Mackenzie's stories tend to leave multiple and sometimes competing impressions on her readers, often allowing for juxtapositions such as sweet and grimy, funny and sad, plain and convoluted—as she see's it, the only way to be honest is to embrace multiplicity and contradiction.

"In the End" pays homage to her interest in historical fiction, which she has been writing since eleven years old, and her curiosity about the fictitious and malleable quality of historical narratives. In the future, Mackenzie hopes to continue using her ever-present imagination as a copywriter and maybe, one day, as author to her very own collection of drawings, stories and poetry.

Sarah Ashton is an English major with a Concentration in Creative Writing at Carleton University. Born and raised in Toronto, she currently lives in Ottawa where she works, studies, and spends too much time and money in coffee shops.

Meryl Baer worked for a financial firm, eventually quitting her job as a financial geek and moving to the New Jersey shore. Blessed with numerous relatives and friends, they visit during the summer. No one stops by in winter, so she writes about her travels and travails, family, food - definitely a passion - and anything else she finds interesting, often with humor. Her work has appeared in anthologies (most recently *Angel Bumps, Feisty After 45, Pure Slush – Happy; Greed*), websites (e.g. - *GRAND Magazine, Sybil Journal, Burning House Press*), and she is a National Society of Newspaper Columnists award winner. Check out her blog, *Six Decades and Counting*: http://sixdecadesandcounting.blogspot.com.

Cassidy Best is a hopeless coffee addict and freelance writer with a penchant for poetry and prose. A self-proclaimed logophile, she exists safely behind observant eyes and writes from a place that draws the ink straight from her own heart. Having found her voice in the written word, she is messily navigating the emotional tumult of a lifelong desire for understanding and connection. She hopes that by sharing this private part of herself, someone in need of a lighthouse may find one.

Roxanne Cardona was born in New York City. She has had poems published in *Animal: A Beast of a Literary Magazine, Commuter Lit, Poetic Medicine, Charleston Anvil*. Forthcoming: *Edison Literary Review, Ethel Zine, Constellations*. She studied with Philip Schultz/Master Class, Writers Studio, NYC for over ten years and currently, Jennifer Franklin, Hudson Valley Writers Center. She has a BA/MS from Hunter College, MS from College of New Rochelle. She was an elementary school teacher and principal in the South Bronx. Roxanne resides in Teaneck, NJ with her husband.

Jennifer Carr lives in Santa Fe, New Mexico with her partner and two children. She is an EMT, Firefighter, Author and Poet. When she is not working at the local hospital or spending time with her family, she spends way too much time reading and writing. Her poetry has been published in print and in many on-line publications. Jennifer loves flying by her own wings and looks for any opportunity to soar to new heights.

Christie Cochrell: Once a New Mexico Young Poet of the Year in Santa Fe, Christie Cochrell now lives and writes by the ocean in Santa Cruz, California. Informed by extensive travel over the years, her writing has been venturing off into international journals (*Belle Ombre*, *The Wild Word*, *Mediterranean Poetry*), but she's happy to have it nesting nearer home as well, in *Birdland Journal* and *The Catamaran Literary Reader*.

Michael Harris Cohen's fiction has won several awards and been published in *Conjunctions*, *Catapult's Tiny Crimes*, *Pseudopod*, *F(r)iction*, *The Dark Magazine*, and *Fanzine*, among other places. He lives with his wife and daughters in Sofia, and teaches Creative Writing and Literature at the American University in Bulgaria. Find him online at Michaelharriscohen.com.

Christine Corrigan: A graduate of Fordham University School of Law and Manhattan College, Christine Shields Corrigan grew up in Staten Island, New York, where she was diagnosed and treated for Hodgkin's lymphoma at fourteen. She built a successful career as a labor and employment law attorney, then as a legal writer and editor.

After surviving cancer again in midlife, Corrigan became a freelance writer, with essays about illness, motherhood, and writing published in *The Brevity Blog*, *Dreamers Creative Writing Year 1 Anthology*, edited by Kat McNichol, *Grown & Flown*, *The Potato Soup Journal*, *Racked.com*, *Ravishly.com*, *Wildfire Magazine*, and elsewhere.

She lives in Somerset County, New Jersey with her husband, three children, and devoted Cavalier King Charles Spaniel. Corrigan serves on the programming committee of the Morristown Festival of Books and teaches creative nonfiction writing for a local adult education program. When she's not writing, Corrigan works in her garden, and enjoys reading and baking, especially pies. Supporting newly diagnosed cancer patients also is an important part of her life.

She recently completed "Again: Surviving Cancer Twice with Love and Lists, A Memoir" and is in the process of seeking to have it published.

Find her at christineshieldscorrigan.com.

Lisa Fleck Dondiego's poems have appeared in *The Sigh Press Literary Journal, The Westchester Review, Haibun Today, Memoir Mixtapes, The Writers' Café*, the Red Moon Press's yearly anthology and in the Contemporary Women Writers of the Hudson Valley's anthology, *A Slant of Light*. Work is forthcoming in *Periwinkle* and the Ecopoetics 2020 special edition of *Dispatches from the Poetry Wars*. Her chapbook, *A Sea Change*, was published by Finishing Line Press in 2011. She lives in Ossining, NY, with her husband.

Jill Evans, also known as Jill Evans Petzall, makes documentary films, media art installations, writes poetry, and teaches about social justice from a female perspective. She is the winner of four Emmy Awards for her scripts and documentary films. She lives in St. Louis, Missouri, and started her career in her 40s while raising three young children as a single mother. All her work is fueled by a graduate degree in Philosophy. Evans focuses on social justice issues, emphasizing how we too easily tell ourselves the wrong stories. Now in her 70s, she has just begun to publish the poetry she has been writing all her life (thus far, her poetry is published in *Tipton Poetry Journal*, *LIGHT a Journal of Photography and Poetry*, *The London Reader*, and *First Literary Review-East*.) A multi-disciplinary artist, she writes poetry to hold life still long enough to be surprised by the meanings in its outlines. Writing poetry has now become her way of life.

Nicholas Forster is a builder of both time and space, crafting homes by day and stories by night. He is the author of such short stories as "Asteroid Adventure", "Ordinary Oliver", and "The Toad". He hopes to complete the A-Z anthology one day; but for now you can check out his *Marine Space* trilogy. Nick hopes to journey beyond the work-a-day world of construction and create his own collected works. His stories explore themes of adventure and heroism, and the possibilities of the human spirit. As Gandalf once said, "We have to decide what to do with the time that is given us," and Nick decides to write.

John Grey is an Australian poet, US resident. Recently published in *Midwest Quarterly, Poetry East* and *North Dakota Quarterly* with work upcoming in *South Florida Poetry Journal, Hawaii Review* and the *Dunes Review.*

Natasha Kirmse is graduate of Carleton University's English and Film programs. Her passion for the English language and the worlds it can create through fiction have guided her interests both personally and academically throughout her life. After being a part of The Writer's Circle's first publication, Natasha is pleased to have her work displayed in the follow-up anthology. Natasha's other published works include children's book *Sam's Shadow* (2007) and her novel *100 Ways to See the World* (2017).

Victoria Klassen holds a Masters in Communications and a Bachelor of Journalism with a double major in English. From a young age she knew that storytelling was her calling. She has spent the last few years writing about mermaids and recently became an open water diver so she could explore the underwater world for herself.

Joseph Murphy has been published in a wide range of print and online journals, including *The Ann Arbor Review, Northwind* and *The Sugar House Review*. He is the author of four poetry collections, *The Shaman Speaks, Shoreline of the Heart, Having Lived* and *Crafting Wings*. Murphy is also a member of the Colorado Authors' League and for eight years (2010–18) was poetry editor for an online literary publication, *Halfway Down the Stairs*.

Brice Peters is a Carleton University honours student with a major in neuroscience and a minor in chemistry. Brice is passionate about writing and this is his second time being published. Brice is a part of the ACACIA fraternity and lives in Ottawa.

Colleen Powderly: "Even to Cry," "The Art Museum at the End of the World," and "The Chair Rider" are from Colleen Powderly's work, *Psalms from an Ordinary Woman*, which is forthcoming in 2020 from Poetry Playhouse Publications. Colleen has also written *Split* (FootHills Publishing, 2009). Her work has appeared in many journals, including *Ekphrasis, Steel Toe Review, Third Wednesday*, and *RiverSedge*, and has been anthologized in *Malala: Poems for Malala Yousefzai* and *Mo' Joe: The Anthology*. Colleen belongs to Just Poets, the premier poetry organization of western New York, and has served on the editorial board for their anthology, *Le Mot Juste*.

Holden Primeau is a correctional officer by day, and aspiring horror novelist by nighttime. He spends his days in New Brunswick with his fantastic wife, two pretty good cats, and two weird dogs.

Logan Primeau is a father, security guard, video game enthusiast, and big fan of shawarma. When he's not streaming the video games that he loves to play, he's thinking of fantastical worlds that he can play around in like a sandbox.

Willy Primeau has a worldly experience in acting, singing, dancing, and many different forms of creative and expressive writing. He started writing at an early age, while he attended high school, and wrote a short one person act titled "A Father's Covenant". He has worked seminars with groups of people, where the focus was on expressive writing and visual art. He is the proud father of four amazing and creative children (thanks, dad) and five wonderful grandchildren. He lives in Ontario with his amazing wife.

Ruth Sabath Rosenthal is a New York poet, well published in the U.S. and, also, internationally. In October 2006, her poem "on yet another birthday" was nominated for a Pushcart Prize by Ibbetson Street Press. Ruth has authored five books: *Facing Home - Facing Home and beyond - little, but by no means small - Food: Nature vs Nurture* and *Gone, but Not Easily Forgotten*. The books can be purchased from Amazon or directly from Ruth, via her website: newyorkcitypoet.com. Her other websites are poetrybyruthsabathrosenthal.com and bigapplepoet.com.

Analisa Salituro is an honours graduate of the University of Toronto's English and Book and Media Studies programs. When she was in high school, her short story "Vertigo" was published in a Penguin short story compilation. When she is not writing, Analisa can be found cooped up in her room binge-watching the latest Netflix show, online shopping, and reading as much as humanly possible.

Vera Salter: Raised in the United Kingdom in a family of refugees from Europe, she moved to the United States in 1969. She holds a PhD in sociology and worked as a healthcare administrator and activist. She writes at the Hudson Valley Writers' Center and has studied with Jennifer Franklin, Amy Holman, Arthur Sze and Patricia Smith. She has been published in *The Five-Two Crime Poetry Weekly*, *Sediments* and *Right Hand Pointing*.

Gerard Sarnat won the Poetry in the Arts First Place Award plus the Dorfman Prize, and has been nominated for a handful of recent Pushcarts plus Best of the Net Awards. Gerry is widely published in academic-related journals (e.g., University Chicago, Stanford, Oberlin, Brown, Columbia, Harvard,

Pomona, Johns Hopkins, Wesleyan, University of San Francisco) plus national (e.g., *Gargoyle, Main Street Rag, New Delta Review, MiPOesias, American Journal Of Poetry, Clementine, pamplemousse, Poetry Quarterly, Free State Review, Poetry Circle, Poets And War, Cliterature, Qommunicate,* Indolent Books, Pandemonium Press, *Texas Review, Brooklyn Review, San Francisco Magazine, The Los Angeles Review* and *The New York Times*) and international publications (e.g., *Review Berlin* and *New Ulster*). He's authored the collections *Homeless Chronicles* (2010), *Disputes* (2012), *17s* (2014), *Melting the Ice King* (2016). Gerry is a physician who's built and staffed clinics for the marginalized as well as a Stanford professor and healthcare CEO. Currently he is devoting energy/resources to deal with global warming. Gerry's been married since 1969 with three kids plus six grandsons, and is looking forward to future granddaughters. gerardsarnat.com

Ann Taylor is a Professor of English at Salem State University in Salem, Mass. where she teaches both literature and writing courses. She has written two books on college composition, academic and free-lance essays, and a collection of personal essays, *Watching Birds: Reflections on the Wing.* Her first poetry book, *The River Within,* won first prize in the 2011 Cathlamet Poetry competition at Ravenna Press. A chapbook, *Bound Each to Each,* was published in 2013. Her most recent collection, published in 2018, *Héloïse and Abélard: the Exquisite Truth* (WordTech Communications), is based on the twelfth-century story of their lives. She is now working on a manuscript entitled, "Sortings".

Blair Urowitz began writing creatively at the age of Seventeen.

She started because her therapist wanted her to put words to her feelings, as she struggled greatly with expressing them. She started writing down sentences, trying to explain any feelings that she had, but none of the pages would make a lot of coherent sense. Through this, she realized that sometimes less is more. She began writing words down that described her feelings and before she knew it, she was creating poems. Through these poems, she was able to dig deeper and open her heart to pain. She began turning this pain into something beautiful, and allowing her pain to be free through artistic expression. She hopes that her poems can help others, the way that they've helped her.

She is currently studying Psychology and Applied Linguistics at Carleton University.

Shelby Van Pelt is a writer of fiction and creative nonfiction. Her most helpful editors are her two cats—that is, when they're not knocking her coffee onto her keyboard. She lives in the Chicago area with her husband and children.

Nathaniel Neil Whelan has an M.A. from Carleton University and a diploma in Professional Writing from Algonquin College. When he is not serving coffee at his local Starbucks, he can be found reading, writing, or buried under a pile of LEGO. He currently lives in Ottawa with his partner and pet cats Goose and Loki.

Laura Wilson was born in Belfast, Northern Ireland and moved to Ottawa with her family when she was nine. She studied accounting at the University of Ottawa and then went on to obtain her accounting designation and started working at Carleton University. She is now following her passion for reading and writing by studying part-time at Carleton in the hopes of obtaining a Bachelor of Arts in English with a specialization in Creative Writing. She is also working on a novel and dreams of filling her days with words instead of numbers.

ABOUT THE EDITORS

Nathan Primeau holds a B.A. in English from Carleton University. He also graduated with a concentration in creative writing, and a minor in film studies. His work has appeared in three DeeBee Publishing anthologies, *Cult Mag*, and the now-defunct *Anthem Little Magazine*. Beyond the work done on the last anthology in *The Writers Circle* series, Nathan has been a reader and blogger for *Ottawa Arts Review*. Nathan lives in Ottawa with his partner and their pets. @nathanprimeau

Abigail Rabishaw is an English major at Carleton University with a concentration in creative writing. Her work has appeared in two anthologies, *Constellations* and *The Stranger Side of Tomorrow*. She has also edited for *Typehouse Literary Magazine*. Abigail lives in Ottawa with her partner (who is also her co-editor), their two dogs, one cat, and 37 houseplants.

DEDICATION

This book is dedicated to all the patient contributors included within that waited as we pushed through this long and harrowing journey into publication. Thank you.

A special thank you goes out to contributors Victoria Klassen, Analisa Salituro, and Nathaniel Neil Whelan. These three chose to volunteer for some of the edits on *The Writers Circle 2* and we are very grateful.